FULL MOON
BLOODY MOON

A Chase Dagger Mystery

Written as Lee Driver

The Chase Dagger Series
The Good Die Twice

Written as S.D. Tooley

The Sam Casey Series
When the Dead Speak
Nothing Else Matters

FULL MOON
BLOODY MOON

A Chase Dagger Mystery

Lee Driver

Full Moon Publishing

Published by
Full Moon Publishing
P.O. Box 408
Schererville, IN 46375
www.mysterypublishers.com

Library of Congress Catalog Number 00-106008
ISBN 0-9666021-4-5   M Y S

10 9 8 7 6 5 4 3 2 1

Published October 2000
Printed in the United States of America

ACKNOWLEDGEMENTS

During the course of this book I have had to pick the brain of the following experts in their field:

George J. Behnle, Jr., Retired Chief Investigator for the Cook County medical examiner; **Mel McNairy** of the Indianapolis Police Department; **Pat Reid**, Director of the Raptor Center at the University of Minnesota College of Veterinary Medicine; **William Sherlock**, User Agency Coordinator for the Illinois State Police Forensic Science Center in Chicago, who not only shared his knowledge of weapons but also let me borrow his name for a character; and **Mark Tilden**, Biophysicist at the Los Alamos National Laboratory.

FULL MOON
BLOODY MOON

1

Monday, October 9, 3:30 a.m.

She didn't have time to scream.

Lisa felt comfortable jogging the Tri-County Lakeshore Trail. Completed last year, it rambled through three Northwest Indiana counties—Lake, Porter, and LaPorte, hugging the southern shores of Lake Michigan. As part of the combined efforts of several towns' tourism bureaus, the Lakeshore Trail succeeded in drawing more sightseers to Indiana beaches, not to mention their gambling boats.

The trail was rarely empty, attracting cyclists, inline skaters, joggers, runners, as well as walkers, at all hours of the day. Except when Lisa jogged. Because of her work schedule, she had to fit in her three-mile jog whenever she could.

The air had a bite to it but she had worked up a sweat so her hooded sweatshirt was tied around her waist. Moonlight glistened off the asphalt path and it was bright enough to see the golden colors of the leaves clinging to the ground.

Blonde hair pulled back in a ponytail bounced across her back. Firm muscles pressed against the spandex pants and there was barely any exertion in Lisa's breathing.

The trail darkened as it ducked through a forest preserve just east of Cedar Point. This was the part of the trail she didn't like, the part where shadows darkened, lurked, appeared to move wantonly. Eyes gleamed from under brush as tiny feet scurried. Shadows appeared to move inward, hiding deeper into the underbrush.

There were two things that calmed Lisa's fears. One was the 9mm Bersa tucked in the holster at the small of her back. The other was Max, her three-year-old Doberman jogging alongside her.

"Here comes the fun part." She tightened her grip on the leash.

The Doberman remained focused. Small animals or even deer were no threat so he ignored them. He was in just as good of shape as his master and neither of them sounded or looked out of breath.

The smell of wet leaves blended with the musty odor of lake waters and residuals of burning leaves to give the air that Midwestern/fall season aroma. This was the time of year when people made their annual trek to the Covered Bridge Festival in southern Indiana to view the best of the fall colors, although Northwest Indiana was no slouch when it came to showing off its finest vibrant shades.

The trail curved inward, cutting deeper into the woods transforming the outdoor path into a shadowy tunnel. Tree branches swayed overhead and leaves rustled as if some of nature's creatures were running to keep up with her.

Max made an abrupt stop, practically pulling Lisa's arm out of its socket. His head jerked up, ears back as he stared at the ceiling of leaves.

"What is it?" Lisa followed his gaze but saw only darkness. The branches were so thick it blocked out any light from the moon. "Come on." She tugged on his leash and continued her jog. There was a clearing ahead where the path opened up. This was Lisa's turn-around point, her halfway mark. The clearing was bathed in moonlight and the young woman felt a sense of relief when she saw several tankers beyond the breakwater, as if proof she wasn't alone in the world. She paused several minutes to take a breather and let Max sniff a few posts. There was something in the way the Doberman kept peering back toward the path that made her uneasy.

Lisa pulled a small flashlight from her pocket. "Come on, Max. Let's go home." The path was bathed in an intense halogen beam. Halfway through the woods the breeze picked up, rustling the trees, sending another flurry of leaves drifting across the asphalt. The high-intensity beam created long shadows and dark pockets and her eyes began to play tricks. And so were her ears. She could swear she heard footsteps on the pavement behind her.

A low growl rumbled from deep within the Doberman's throat. His entire body turned and skidded as though on ice. The high beam reflected off the pavement but as far as the beam reached, the path was empty.

It took a lot to make Lisa nervous. Seeing Max bare his teeth, hearing his growl intensify, caused her heart to pound against her rib cage. This wasn't just a wild rabbit or fox.

Something was out there. Peering at the shadows ahead, Lisa dropped the leash and moved the flashlight to her left hand. Slowly, she reached around for her Bersa.

"What is it? What do you see?" she whispered. Her heartbeat pounded in her ears and a chill shuddered through her body. Branches bucked and swayed, fighting a useless battle to keep their foliage. Another thrashing overhead brought Max's head around, ears straight up, another low growl.

"Max?" Lisa heard a thud behind her, as though the wind had knocked down a tree limb, sending it crashing to the ground.

Max jerked and turned quickly. Lisa followed suit, her left hand pointing the beam of light toward her attacker. Suddenly, a force knocked the flashlight from her hand as Max let out a high-pitched whine. All Lisa had noticed before the flashlight was extinguished were two yellow eyes, glowing like large slitted moons. At first, he was twenty feet away but he covered the distance between them so quickly that Lisa thought he either drifted or was flying. Her fingers felt for the butt of her gun. The ground dropped from under her yet she could still see him in front of her. She soon realized she was being lifted and her attacker was rising with her. Such power, such swiftness. How could this be happening? She didn't feel any pain. Why not? Was this some type of animal whose venom rendered her paralyzed? She couldn't feel her arms much less move her fingers. All she felt was a warmth spreading over her chest. She thought it might have been fear that created that sensation. But then realized it was her own blood spilling down the front of her shirt. Where was it coming from?

Everything had happened in the blink of an eye. Lisa didn't have time to think. Didn't have time to defend herself. Didn't have time to pull out her gun.

She didn't have time to scream.

October 9, 4:35 a.m.

Do you wanna have some fun?

Dagger's eyes flew open. The voice came from some-where, everywhere. He blinked the sleep from his eyes and tried to get his bearings. A canopy over the bed, sheer drapes covering the windows, eyelet pillow cases. This definitely wasn't his bedroom. Slowly he sat up, noticing a partially clad body facing away from him.

"God, what the hell?" He ran his hands through his long hair and shook the cobwebs from his head. He had stopped off for a couple drinks and ran into his ex-fiancee. The last place he wanted to end up was in Sheila's bed. Checking his body he saw that he still had his clothes on. Relieved, he remembered he had driven Sheila home because she had too much to drink. Then she had wanted him to stay until she fell asleep. Mr. Nice Guy. He had to change his persona if he wanted to discourage her.

Dagger, are you awake?

14

The voice again. This time he recognized where it was coming from—inside his head.

Sara, where are you? He stood and stretched his lean body, searched in the dark for his shoes, tried not to make any noise and risk waking up the blonde witch on wheels.

Do you remember Padre mentioning the ATF was on the lookout for a shipment of illegal weapons?

Dagger stumbled through the dark living room, stepped into his shoes, and grabbed his jacket.

Yeah, something in the multi-millions I think he said. He patted his jacket pocket for his keys but they weren't there. It would be just like Sheila to hide them so he couldn't leave. There was something about Sheila's condo he didn't like. The décor for one. Too white, too clean-looking. Too damn expensive. Barely even needed a nightlight with all the white furniture lighting up the room like huge glow cushions.

Well, guess what?

Dagger smiled at the excitement in Sara's voice. *What?* He lifted the lid on a silver candy dish but his keys weren't there either.

I'm by a warehouse near the harbor. I think it used to be a brewery. There are guys here unloading crates from a semi. They dropped one and it broke open. I got close enough to read HK69A1 40MM.

He almost dropped the lid onto the glass top table. *Jezzus, that's a goddam Heckler & Koch grenade launcher.* Again he checked his jacket, pulled a pen light from his pocket, and checked the drawers in the end tables, the cubbie holes in the Queen Anne secretary. Then he found

Sheila's purse on one of the wing-backed chairs.

Should we call Padre?

Sergeant Jerry Martinez was known as Padre to close friends because of the brief time he had spent in the seminary before joining the police force. He was one of the few people Dagger trusted.

I'll do that. Dumping the contents of the purse on the chair, Dagger quickly found his keys. "Bitch," he said under his breath. He fled the condo feeling as if he were escaping a fate worse than death. Sure sign that it wasn't true love, which was why he had broken off the engagement in the first place.

Climbing into his black Lincoln Navigator, he started it up and turned on the heat. *What's happening now, Sara?*

They are carrying the crates inside. I'm on the roof looking through a broken vent window. You wouldn't believe the number of crates, Dagger.

Must have brought them in by boat. Dagger tucked his long hair under a black baseball cap, then punched the autodial button for Padre's home phone and steered the Navigator out of the parking lot. After three rings, the phone was answered.

"This better be good. I'm on vacation," the groggy voice said.

"It will be worth it, Padre."

"Dagger?"

Dagger could hear the rustling of sheets and lumbered breathing.

"I think I found that shipment of weapons ATF is looking for."

"What?" Padre's response was a loud whisper.

Dagger listened as Padre called his office on another phone. Flipping open the cooler in the console, he pulled out a bottle of water and wished it were a steaming hot cup of coffee. Next, he punched a button on the dashboard and a screen came to life. It lit up a cool gray with a grid of the city. A red blip pulsed. It was a tracking device so he knew where Sara was at all times. The sensor was in a small earring clamped to the top of her right ear. When she shifted into the hawk or wolf, the earring looked as if the animal were tagged. If something happened to Sara in her shifted form, if she lost consciousness and was unable to communicate with him telepathically, he would be able to locate her.

They aren't unloading everything, Dagger.

What are they doing?

They left two men at the warehouse. The rest are in the truck with the remaining crates.

Smart. They aren't stashing them in the same location. I'm not far from the warehouse, Sara. Follow the truck and let me know where it goes.

Dagger relayed the information to Padre, then turned down Lake Street. It was a frontage-type road, which ran the length of the beach. He parked the Navigator alongside a boat storage facility. Tarp-covered power boats and sail boats were in the process of being readied for winter. Dagger killed the headlights and rolled down the dark-tinted driver's side window. His night-vision binoculars revealed very little activity below at the warehouse. Doors were closed, windows blocked, no guards outside. Padre's posse was only a few minutes away. Dagger stole a quick glance at the screen to see the location of the red blinking light.

The gray hawk glided over the treetops, its forty-inch wing span silhouetted against the moonlit sky. Even from this altitude it could read the license plate number of the truck heading east. The driver was avoiding the entrance ramp to the toll road and turning south instead, away from well-monitored expressways.

If the truck had stayed on an easterly course, the hawk might have detected something else. It might have sensed danger, smelled the strong scent of life blood, discovered a sight more gruesome than it had ever seen before.

3

October 9, 9:05 a.m.

Sara reached for her glass of orange juice, then hesitated. Her eyes searched the dark area rug from the doorway to the couch. Nothing escaped her keen eyesight. She took a swallow of juice while watching for movement. With a shrug, she set her glass down and settled back against the couch cushions, the morning paper across her lap. A yard of sun-streaked hair streamed down her arms. She gathered it to one side and quickly created a long braid.

Morning light sliced through the wall of windows, showcasing a sprawling landscape bursting with fall colors. Sara felt safe from the outside world here on three hundred acres of reservation land. It was nestled on the eastern edge of Cedar Point, a suburb of Indiana. The mausoleum of a building with its multitude of skylights resembled a research lab or planetarium more than a residence.

Again something dark scurried across the carpeting and under the oak coffee table. Pulling her feet up under her, she leaned over and peered around the table. Although she detested spiders, she always told herself they were only lost. She would usually capture them in a glass and release them outside. Roaches were a different story. Other than dust floating through the shafts of light, she saw little evidence of anything else moving.

Puzzled, she straightened, her gaze drifting to the shadows under the bookcases and dark corners by Dagger's desk. Still not convinced, Sara slowly rolled the newspaper into a weapon, ready to strike if it were a roach. Another movement caught her eye, this time on the couch, scurrying toward her from the armrest. It was black, about the size of a quarter with gleaming red eyes.

"AIYEEEH." Sara leaped from the couch and threw the rolled up paper toward the insect. "DAGGER!" She screamed as she fell back on her rump. Her feet and hands back-pedaled away from the pursuing beast as it leaped from the couch and charged after her.

She heard laughter drifting from the doorway to Dagger's bedroom. Her turquoise eyes flashed anger at her partner, who was doubled over, tears in his eyes.

"DO SOMETHING!"

A blur of scarlet and blue flew over to the aviary door. Sara's screams had awakened Einstein who clamped his claws onto the grates. "HELP ME, HELP ME!" Einstein screeched.

"I am doing something," Dagger laughed as he worked the remote in his calloused hands. Amusement sparked a light in his dark eyes. He dropped to one knee and held his hand on the floor, palm up. The black object crawled onto it.

"What is that?" Sara followed Dagger to the couch.

"WHAT'S THAT? AWWWKK." The scarlet macaw clamped its beak onto the grating and climbed higher. "OUT, OUT," Einstein demanded.

Dagger set the spider on the coffee table and handed her the remote. "Want to try?"

"Where did you get this?" She cautiously pressed the lever and watched the spider scurry. It flew off the table, landed on the floor, righted itself and turned. Sara laughed as she reached down to retrieve the metal object. "Did Skizzy make this?"

"We both worked on it. Unique, isn't it?" He scratched the rough stubble on his chin. They hadn't returned home until five in the morning and barely slept. The high from the weapons bust still had the adrenaline pulsing through his veins. Dagger had stayed in the comfort of his SUV while Padre, the ATF and SWAT teams descended on the ware-house. According to Padre, the state police had intercepted the semi near Griffith, Indiana.

Sara studied the gadget. Its body was glistening ebony with four legs. Beady red eyes were separated by a square, micron-sized reflector. Turning it over, she found a hard metal underside. There was barely any weight to it.

Dagger was amazed at her unusual curiosity. He couldn't have asked for a better partner in Dagger Investigations. The business was located in Sara's house and he rented office and living space for himself and Einstein. Sara's room was at the top of the steel staircase at the end of the catwalk. The rent he paid in addition to her salary as his partner gave Sara the money she needed to maintain her grandparents' house. The arrangement Dagger had with Sara fit perfectly. It had been an unspoken promise he had made to Sara's grandmother before she died that he would watch out for her eighteen-year-old granddaughter. Keep her safe in a world that was as foreign to her as she was to the world.

"Batteries, right?" Sara asked, holding the spider between her fingers.

"No. It actually uses a microcore controller. Absorbs its energy from a light source."

"Sunlight?"

"And lamps, even the glow from a TV. Skizzy calls it LEMICC. Light energized microcore controller. Just MICK for short."

"Mick." Sara smiled revealing the most perfect set of lips known to mankind. "Neat. What do you use him for?"

Dagger took the spider from her and pointed between its red eyes. "Audio and visual surveillance. There's a small camera right there."

"What is the range?"

"Skizzy and I both have receivers. We figure we can cover a twenty-mile radius." He raked his fingers through his shaggy hair and stretched. "Weren't you going shopping?"

Sara checked the clock on the wall above Dagger's desk. The mall had opened thirty minutes ago.

He grabbed her wrist as she stood. "Are you sure you're up to this?"

She nodded, mustering as much self-confidence as she could. "Yes. I'll be fine."

An hour after Sara left, the buzzer at the front gate sounded.

"AWK, COMPAN," Einstein announced.

Dagger pressed the button to open the wrought iron gate at the entrance to the long drive. With a devilish smile, he set the spider under the coffee table and slipped the remote in his pocket.

Less than a minute later, Dagger opened the front door to a burly black man.

"PLEASE MR. POSTMAN. AWK." Einstein spread his brightly colored wings and settled on his perch.

Simon gave a wave toward Einstein and rubbed a beefy hand across his chin. He walked over to the Florida room and peered in. "Got them paddle fans installed. Lookin' good." Simon rubbed his foot against the stone quarry tiled floor. The addition was roomy, at least five-hundred-square feet. Jalousie windows were cranked open creating a pleasant breeze. "This must have set you back a pretty penny. You didn't charge that sweet thing for all this work, did you?"

"Nah. I look at it as part of my room and board."

Simon admired the variety of plants and bright floral cushioned chairs. "At least Sara added color to this place. You and that black and gray you always wear is like livin' in a goddam silent movie." He tossed a glance at Dagger's black denim pants and black shirt and lifted his eyebrows as if to prove a point. "Be even better once she gets rid of that black furniture you got in the living room."

Dagger's fingers played with the buttons on the remote. Simon's back was to the couch so he didn't see the black object charging across the area rug, its red eyes gleaming in the sunlight. But once it hit the quarry tile, the tap-tapping of its metal legs made Simon jerk his head around. His eyes bulged, resembling hard-boiled eggs with giant Milk Duds in the center.

Simon screamed, "Holy shit," lifted his foot, and slammed a heavy boot down against the ensuing bug.

Sinking against the door jamb, Dagger shook his head. "Who says old men don't have good reflexes."

"If it's movin', I'm stompin'." Simon bent down closer, hands on his knees, as Dagger used a pencil to separate the pieces.

"You killed Mick." Dagger picked the metal pieces up in his hand and stood.

"What the hell is a Mick?" Simon peered into the palm of Dagger's hand. When Dagger pulled the remote from his pocket and showed it to his friend, Simon started laughing, a deep jovial laugh that jiggled the belly hanging over his belt buckle. "You got a goddam baby robot there?"

Dagger slid the pieces into an envelope. "I'll give the parts to Skizzy. It was just the prototype." He sealed the envelope and tossed it on his desk.

Simon wiped the tears from his cherub cheeks. "Ain't that a hoot. Where you gonna use them?"

"In the words of Skizzy, 'anywhere we damn well please.'" A smile played across his lips as he told Simon how he had scared the daylights out of Sara earlier.

"AWK, AWK. KILL IT KILL IT." Einstein poked his beak through the grating.

Dagger closed the Plexiglas soundproof door to the

aviary reducing the loud screeching from Einstein. The macaw was thirty-six inches of bold coloring. He had been payment for one of Dagger's P.I. jobs. Just never got around to taking him to the zoo or placing an ad in the papers. But macaws can be rather noisy and it was difficult finding an apartment let alone office space that would tolerate Einstein.

Simon set Dagger's stack of mail on the coffee table and settled onto the loveseat. Running one envelope under his nose, he inhaled deeply. "Ummmm. Smells like pretty expensive perfume." He dangled the envelope from his fingertips. "Must be close to Sweetest Day."

Dagger sank down onto the worn leather couch, suddenly feeling the lack of sleep. He grabbed the envelope from Simon, checked the handwriting, and tossed the card on the coffee table. "I did something stupid last night." He told Simon how he had helped a drunken Sheila home and tucked her in.

"I'm sure she wasn't faking it." Simon scoffed, a reaction from someone who knew women like Sheila. "Hope you didn't do anything you'd regret later."

"No. At least I don't think so."

"You'd remember that. Trust me. Must be tough being stalked by a women who is NOT the love of your life." Simon's gaze circled the room, followed the steel staircase to the second floor. Finally, he said, "Speaking of the love of your life, where is Sara?"

"Can't you ever walk in here without insinuating…" Dagger pressed the palms of his hands to his eyes. "I may as well be talking to a brick wall. Sara's a child. She's like my little sister."

"Uh huh, uh huh." Simon settled back against the couch cushions, hands clasped behind his head. He had a perpetual little-boy grin, the one his wife always said was a sign that he was up to no good. Always the tease, Simon never passed up an opportunity to rib his friend about his love life. "I'm sure being the great detective you are you noticed the birth date on her drivers license. That supposed child is going to be nineteen in a couple months."

"Sara has a birthday?"

"Most people do."

"You know what I mean." Dagger made a mental note to ask Skizzy the exact date of Sara's birthday. After all, it was Skizzy who had prepared all of Sara's I.D.s.

"I just remember her mentioning her birthday was close to Christmas."

One small detail Dagger neglected to find out about his partner. Less personal information he knew, the safer it was. But that was a joke. No one knew Sara better than Dagger.

"What else is happening in town, besides the ATF raid?"

"Mean you didn't hear?" Simon was better than the old time switchboard operators. He loved being the one in the know. "Two joggers found a body on Lakeshore Trail."

"Drowning?"

Simon shook his head. "Stabbing." Simon stood and wobbled over to the desk in a rolling gait, as if his legs weren't strong enough to carry his massive torso. "The body was hangin' from a limb twenty feet off the ground."

Twenty feet. Dagger's mind was already beginning to calculate the distance.

"Have they I.D.'d the victim?"

Simon shook his head. "Cops are very hush hush about this one."

"Well, Padre's on vacation so I doubt he'll be working the case." Dagger stood and stretched, checked his watch. "Sara was brave today and decided to go to the mall."

"Uh oh," Simon shook his head. "Bad day. They got that classic auto show at the mall. Expecting eighty thousand plus people."

"Shit!"

4

October 9, 10:18 a.m.

"Damn. I'm on vacation. Hasn't anyone ever heard that term before?" Padre mumbled as he walked the grid again, squatting down every few feet to look for pieces of evidence the murderer might have left behind. A murderer always leaves something and takes something. Rule of thumb. It might be a thread, a hair, a fingerprint, footprint, saliva. But this was a puzzler. He straightened and stared at the body being lowered from the tree. A hush fell over the clusters of Crime Scene techs and fellow cops, as though in tribute to a fallen comrade.

How the hell did she get up that high, Padre asked himself. There wasn't any reason she should have been left hanging there that long. But the chief wanted this case handled with kid gloves. Wanted the Crime Scene Unit to leave no stone unturned and the grid walked for hours before the body was removed. All procedures had to be followed to the letter. No cutting corners. This one was classified HSC-highly sensitive case.

The press had been kept at bay a half-mile away and given a simple press release stating a young woman had been stabbed. Time of the murder was estimated between three-thirty and five in the morning. The victim's name was Lisa Cambridge. Lisa had been a member of the Cedar Point Police Department.

Padre stared past the yellow crime scene tape where Chief John Wozniak stood. Red-faced, red hair, a bulbous schnozz filling out his face. His aunt always told him noses that size could be used to snuff out the candles in church. Like Padre, John had attended Saint Michael's School and even entered the seminary around the same time. Padre had found police work more to his liking. John found women more to his liking. He had been married three times.

As the body was placed on the gurney, Padre was shocked at the slice across the woman's neck. But what surprised him even more was when Luther, the county medical examiner, untied the sweatshirt from around Lisa's waist. Shaking his head, Padre walked over to where Chief Wozniak stood. The sun dodged between the clouds and a damp breeze flirted with his thinning hairline.

"You won't believe this, Chief. Lisa had her gun on her. And the safety was still on." Padre turned and watched as Luther bagged the gun and handed it to a Crime Scene tech.

"Make sure the scumbag didn't place it there. I find it hard to believe she didn't fire her gun. And where is her Doberman? She never jogged without him," Wozniak said.

"My men are combing the area now for the dog. Lisa didn't get off work until three and usually jogged right after.

Body was found around six." Padre gazed at the crime scene again. "This is a mess. What blood wasn't soaked up in the ground was instead soaked by the leaves which were then blown from here to kingdom come."

John's trench coat flapped in the breeze and he pulled the collar up around his neck. Settling his hat on his head, he turned toward Padre. "Sorry about the vacation, Martinez. I'll make it up to you."

"No problem." Padre rubbed the bridge of his nose where a small bump reminded him every day of his fight with Merle the Moose in high school. Only time he ever had a broken nose. Padre was stocky, around five-foot-ten, but never shied away from a good fight. Now he preferred fighting twenty-pound salmon on the end of a fishing line. Which brought him back to pining for the fishing cottage up in Michigan where he was supposed to be right now.

"And about that other problem. You said you had someone you could talk to about it?"

Padre replied, "I have just the man for the job."

"Good. You report to me and only me." John shoved his hands deep into the pockets of his London Fog. "Great bust last night. I don't know who your informant is but he's worth every penny."

Padre smiled. "Somehow I always end up owing him."

John jerked his head toward the parking lot. "What about Lisa's boyfriend?"

Padre studied the tall black man pacing in front of the M.E. wagon. J.D. was also a Cedar Point cop. A bruiser of a guy, shaved head, all muscle packed in a linebacker-sized body. He and Lisa had been living together for the past two years.

"I don't think he had anything to do with it."

"He found the body."

"Only because he knew where Lisa jogged and she wasn't home when he got up this morning."

"No witness that he was at home, was there?"

Padre shook his head. "When it came to Lisa, he was a gentle giant."

John gave the big man a cursory stare. "Would take a big man to pull a body up that high."

"There was no blood anywhere on that tree, Chief." Padre gazed again at J.D. who was sitting on the bumper of his Chevy Blazer, staring at the lake, obviously trying to avoid looking at the body bag being carried to the M.E. wagon.

"He could have knocked her out, carried her up the tree, wedged her body between the limbs."

Padre lit a cigarette, took a long drag, flicked the match away. "And with his weight, he's going to bend over that limb, slit her throat and then climb down?"

Chief Wozniak stared at the area where Lisa's body had been suspended. The branches were wishboned and her body had been wedged in so tight they had to cut the limb from the tree by using a fire department snorkel.

"This one's for the books, Chief," Padre said.

A tall man appeared in front of the sergeant's desk at the Indianapolis Police Department and set a briefcase on the corner. "Came as fast as I could."

Marty looked around the office. Curious stares had followed the man into the room. With a nod of his head he said, "Let's talk over here, Bill."

Sergeant Marty Flynn grabbed a file folder from his bottom drawer and his cup of coffee from the desk and led the professor to a conference room. The door closed with a click and he stared for some length at the youthful looking man with the streaks of white running through his hair. Bill opened his briefcase, pulled out his laptop and switched it on. Then he took out a thick notepad, which was divided in sections by dates.

"This one looks good," Marty announced. "Call came in this morning from Cedar Point. Victim had her throat slit and was found suspended from a limb more than twenty feet off the ground." He sat across from the professor and took a swig of hot coffee. "Do you think it's possible it stayed here in the area? In the Midwest?"

The younger man's fingers flew across the keyboard. "I've entered every homicide across the states around a Friday the thirteenth since March of ninety-eight. I knew the closer we got to October thirteenth the worse it would get." He looked up from his keyboard, the lines etched around his eyes revealing a man who had slept very little lately. "It's only the ninth of October. If it's that brutal now, what's it going to be like on Friday?"

Marty's hand trembled as he brought the cup to his mouth. He checked his watch. Almost noon. "I know a guy on the force in Cedar Point. Good guy. Can keep his mouth shut. A: 1 god knows, we don't need any publicity on this."

* * *

The man stopped his bike at the designated spot under the viaduct. Low clouds were rolling in, pushed by a westerly breeze, promising afternoon showers. Swinging his leg over the back, he popped the kickstand and unhooked the straps of the saddlebag.

"Got the goods?" A figure in a hooded sweatshirt and dark sunglasses stood in the shadows.

"Got the package?" The man walked toward the concrete wall. He stopped and watched as a family pedaled past. Once the path was clear he pulled the package from the bag and set it on the ground. Never once looking at who was standing in the shadows, he picked up the envelope that was tossed in front of him, stuffed it in his saddlebag and continued his ride. All in a day's work.

Dagger had circled the mall for several minutes before he found her. Simon was right. The classic auto show came every year to Cedar Creek Mall and packed in car enthusiasts that would shame even the busiest Christmas shopping day.

The closest parking space he found was across the inner drive so he parked his Navigator and walked toward the entrance between Field's and the food court. Fall flowers were in bloom, filling the areas under the trees near the entrances. The management spared little expense in maintaining the outside as well as inside mall areas. And mall security was strict and plentiful, making sure area thieves knew the mall had the lowest crime rate in the Midwest.

Wooden park benches rested under the shade of the trees, and it was on one of these benches that Sara sat, staring straight ahead through dark aviator sunglasses, her hair draping past the hem of her plum-colored leather jacket.

Dagger hung back, studied her for a while. She had been here for almost two hours. Had she even ventured into the mall? He could imagine her driving his truck, finally feeling comfortable using a stick shift, and filled with all kinds of confidence that she could handle a somewhat crowded mall, at least more crowded than at ten o'clock, when it first opened. And then he could imagine her fear when she saw the packed lot and the hordes of people. She probably had been rooted to that same spot since she arrived.

He was just ready to approach when Sara stood, fists clenched, that determined firmness in her jaw. As she turned in the direction of the mall entrance, several clusters of shoppers descended, brushing past her, joining others as tight groups erupted from the building amid shouting and laughter.

Sara backed away, her hand feebly clutching for the armrest of the bench as she shakily lowered herself back down. Dagger expected it wouldn't be long until one of her knuckles found its way to her mouth, a nervous habit that left Sara's knuckles red and bleeding.

Just when he had thought she made progress with feeling comfortable in public, something like this would happen. She was frozen in that one spot, unable to just turn and walk back to the truck. But he could tell by the set of her jaw that she was bound and determined to not let her fears win.

Dagger also noticed several admirers, young men sitting on one of the benches under another tree, and others standing several feet behind her, like packs of hyenas waiting to pounce. Sara always drew stares. When she had stood, he noticed she was wearing a sweater that barely reached her waist, and low riding plum-colored denim pants, exposing a firm and tan midriff. He could only assume she put on the sunglasses to hide the tears in her eyes. If she hadn't worn the glasses, they would have immediately noticed her exotic beauty, the high cheekbones and blue-green eyes. He suddenly wished he hadn't exposed her to fashion magazines and let her stay in her baggy, homemade sack dresses that covered all of her attributes.

Simon's words kept ringing in his head. Dagger had a terrible habit of ridiculing Sara when she had one of her panic attacks, of calling her a baby. And Simon warned him to have more patience with her. After all, she had led a very secluded life. Even her grandmother had never left the three hundred acres except to sell her home-grown vegetables and canned goods at a self-built farm stand at the entrance to their property.

Patience. A word Dagger struggled with a lot. But he was getting better. And there was no better time than now to rescue Sara since the boys in heat were starting to circle, getting ready to make their move. Dagger could see it in their eyes.

Slowly, Dagger strode over to the bench and casually sat down next to Sara. He pulled off his sunglasses, rubbed them on the front of his shirt and leaned over, forearms on his knees, glasses dangling from his fingertips.

"Not quite the perfect day to go shopping." Dagger stared straight ahead at the young men with lust in their eyes. Sara said nothing. "I wouldn't even attempt to shop during the classic auto show. It's more wall-to-wall people than the Friday after Thanksgiving." Still no response from Sara. He glanced over at her hands, the fingers white from being clasped tightly.

Finally, Sara said, "That's still no excuse. It shouldn't have bothered me."

"Don't beat yourself up."

"Easy for you to say," she snapped.

One of the boys in heat made a move. He turned up the collar on his leather jacket. Acting Mister Tough Guy in front of his friends. Dagger wanted to pull on the ring piercing the guy's eyebrow.

"He bothering you, Miss?" Mister Tough Guy asked Sara.

Dagger glared at him, his glasses still dangling. "Get lost."

"I wasn't talking to you."

Dagger stood, towering over the fresh-faced kid with the body piercing and the country club emblem on his shirt. Rich kid. Probably drove a Porsche and golfed at Daddy's prestigious country club. Dagger did not exactly cut a figure anyone would want to mess with. His dark eyes were brooding, deep set, and when he wasn't turning on his warm smile for Sara, he could exude danger from every pour of his body. With his dark hair, continuous five-o-clock shadow, and deep summer tan, he could easily be mistaken for a terrorist and denied boarding on international flights.

He glared at the youth long enough for the sweat to start forming at the kid's hairline. Dagger said, "I sure hope you weren't talking to her."

Sara grabbed his arm. "Dagger, please."

"She doesn't look fine to me." He was brave now. Back-up arrived. His friends had moved off the bench and joined him.

Dagger blinked slowly, his deep inset eyes never wavering from the youth's. Dagger was lean but what his quilted vest hid was a well-toned body and a 3.15-inch barrel Kimber .45 snapped into the holster at the small of his back, not that he would flash his gun in public. He had a better weapon.

"She's my sister," Dagger announced. If there was anything that deflated a young man's testosterone level, it was hearing that someone was a girl's father or brother. Fathers and brothers were territorial. It didn't matter that it wasn't true. The boys in heat believed it. And they backed down.

As they quietly retreated, Dagger sank back down onto the bench. He lifted Sara's sunglasses and peered at her red eyes, dropped the glasses back in place.

"We all have good days and bad. Did the truck stall at all today?"

Sara shook her head no.

"See," he smiled, a warm smile that softened his features. "So another day you'll probably conquer the mall but the truck will die on you." He slid his sunglasses back on the bridge of his nose. "I haven't had lunch yet and that new Rain Forest Café you wanted to try just opened. I think the least you can do after keeping me out so late last night is to buy me lunch."

That brought the hint of a smile to her lips. Dagger rose and held out his hand. She grabbed it and stood. Wrapping an arm around her shoulder, he kissed the top of her head. And he smiled to himself as they walked to the parking lot. What he loved most were the barbs he was feeling, the green eyes of envy leveled at his back.

5

October 9, 12:05 p.m.

Dagger checked the beeper clamped to his belt and pulled out his cell phone. Padre answered on the third ring.

"What happened to your vacation?" Dagger asked.

"A homicide has a way of interrupting those slices of relaxation. Where are you? We gotta talk."

Dagger told him the name of the restaurant and hung up. Sara sat across from him, her eyes wide in amazement at the automated animals, the mock thunderstorm and lightning, the sounds of drizzling rain. He could tell she felt completely relaxed in this atmosphere. They were at a table near a saltwater fish tank containing some of the most unusual fish either of them had ever seen. Overhead, a literal rain forest of foliage hung with automated parrots and other unusual species chattering away.

"Like the place?" He combed his hair back with his fingers and wrapped a rubber band around the thick, shoulder-length hair.

Sara's smile radiated. "It's wonderful." Her eyes were expressive and reflected the curiosity and innocence of her youth but in some respects she had the maturity and intellect beyond her eighteen years.

While they studied their menus, Dagger told her about Padre's phone call.

"He's coming here?"

"Yes. He didn't say what he wanted."

The restaurant started to fill and was soon a buzz of activity, between the clatter of dishes, random conversations, and laughter of children. They no sooner placed their order then Sergeant Martinez arrived.

"How do you like my fishing outfit?" He slipped out of his trench coat and did a three-hundred-and-sixty-degree turn, showing off his dark suit, white shirt, and tie. "Pretty good, huh?" He threw the coat over the back of his chair and sat down. "Let me order first and I'll be right with you." He flagged down a waitress and ordered a thick burger and side salad. "And keep the coffee coming, sweetheart," Padre added.

"Well, well. If it isn't my two favorite men." Sheila slid one arm across Dagger's shoulder. With a well-lacquered nail, she pushed her platinum hair behind one ear. She always used her left hand for this well-practiced movement so she could show the world her engagement ring, a ring that should have been taken off months ago. But Sheila still held out hope. With a flirtatious wink to Padre she slid one hip onto the chair next to Dagger.

"If I didn't know better, Miss Monroe, I'd say you've been following me." Padre winked back at her.

"Missed you this morning." Her hand trailed off of Dagger's shoulder and down his arm.

Sara watched the theatrics unfolding. There wasn't a hair out of place on Sheila's head. Sara had seen clothes like Sheila's in the more expensive stores in the mall. Most of the clientele were dropped off my chauffeured limousines. And one of the hotels had an exclusive salon where the rich socialites had their bodies fussed over, their hair colored and styled. Sara would usually stand in the window and just watch how the women looked when they walked in and the transformation as they walked out.

Sheila's skin was flawless, make-up picture perfect, a trim model-sized body. She was beautiful. And she knew it. And it wasn't unusual for Dagger's ex-fiancee to ignore Sara as she was doing now.

"I don't suppose you are going to discuss the murder this morning," Sheila said.

"I'm sure *The Daily Herald* would love to get all the scoop." Dagger lifted Sheila's hand from his arm and placed it on the table.

Sheila's father, Leyton Monroe owned *The Daily Herald*, along with a laundry list of other publications across the U.S.

The waitress set a pot of coffee in front of Padre. He filled his cup saying, "Now why would I want to give a statement to *The Daily Herald's* ace reporter? Seeing that all statements are coming only from the office of the police chief, I really think you are wasting your time, little lady." He blew at the steam wafting from his cup.

"Just wanted a few comments off the record. Can you

blame a girl?" Sheila placed her handbag on the table and stood. "Maybe you can think about it for a few minutes while I go powder my nose."

Padre waited until Sheila was out of range before saying, "We've got a problem at Headquarters."

Sara stared at Sheila's leather handbag. Her eyebrows scrunched as if pondering a major problem. Not only was she curious why the handbag was left, she was also puzzled by the whirring sound she was hearing. "Why would she powder her nose and leave her purse?" Sara asked Dagger.

Dagger stared at the pink leather clutch bag. Curious, he unfastened the clasp. Inside he found a micro-sized tape recorder set on RECORD.

Padre grabbed the recorder from him and spoke into it. "Miss Monroe, I am sure you are aware tape recording conversations without prior knowledge is against the law." He pressed the STOP button and shook his head. "I have no use for reporters."

Dagger placed the recorder back in Sheila's purse and glanced over at Sara. "Good work."

The waitress brought their food and they ate while Padre talked.

"We removed the cameras in the evidence room and installed one of those new-fangled fingerprint scans. The gizmo cost big bucks," he said around a wad of French fries, "but in the long run, it's supposed to save money. No clerk needed, blah blah. Well," he took a sip of coffee, "seems one of the guns we took off the bozo guarding the warehouse last night was logged into the Evidence Room six months ago. Now it's suddenly in his possession."

"How long ago was the scanner installed?"

"Two months. They did an inventory before it was installed and the HK carbine was there. Did an inventory last week, the damn thing comes up checked out."

Dagger's eyebrows shot up. "Carbine?" He watched Sara pick around several items in her grilled salmon salad. He peered over at her plate. "Those are garbanzo beans, Sara."

She shot him a look over her fork but it was too late for him to reel the words back in. He should have learned his lesson after the last social function he dragged her to. Sara had taken a sip of her soup and whispered across the table to him, "My soup is cold." Dagger had replied that it was vichyssoise, it was supposed to be cold. Unfortunately, rather than whispering he had responded in a normal tone that could be heard by everyone seated at the table in the swank Le Bistro Restaurant. This brought chuckles from the Tylers and Monroes. Sheila had taken the opportunity to blurt out, "For godsake. Can't you take her to a McDonald's?" Sara had never tasted vichyssoise before and didn't know there were soups that were supposed to be served cold. Favorite foods eaten by the rich and famous were not on her list of Internet research subjects.

Dagger had apologized profusely that night but dug his grave even more the next day by giving her a book on gourmet eating. Sheila had suggested it. He should have known better than to think Sheila had Sara's or his best interests in mind.

"They don't have much of a taste to them." Dagger shrugged apologetically, still not knowing when to leave well enough alone.

"Hate it when they add strange stuff to my food," Padre said. "Just lettuce and tomato. Maybe some cucumber. But leave that grassy stuff out and the sunflower seeds and any other foo-foo crap."

To Padre, Dagger said, "Without a clerk at the desk, how do you verify what left the room?"

"There are tags on each item that have to be scanned. We don't have a problem finding out who took it. It's all in the scan log. The problem is the guy retired three months ago. Lou Riley is living out in Idaho."

"You talked to him?"

"Talked to his daughter."

"When's the last time he was in town?"

"She hasn't seen him since he left. He does a lot of hunting. Planned a trip to Canada, Alaska, she wasn't sure when he would be calling next."

"But she's sure he left town?"

"Positive."

The thunder and lightning show drowned out their conversation. Dagger pushed his plate away and watched Sara's eyes scan the ceiling. Children at a nearby table ran over to where the elephant heads were moving. The waitress came by and asked Dagger if they wanted dessert. They declined.

Once the noise quieted down, Padre continued. "Anyway, it's an inside job. That's for sure. And to really confuse things, the same guy took out five other pieces since he supposedly retired."

Dagger tented his hands and propped them under his chin. He stared at the fish tank in thought, watched the fish darting in and out of the sunkin' ship and mock log resting on the bottom of the tank, while he mulled possibilities around in his head.

"Someone take a copy of his fingerprints from the file and use it?" Dagger asked.

Padre shook his head. "Scanner is too sensitive. Would pick up on the paper, know it wasn't authentic." He pushed his chair away from the table, crossed one ankle over his knee. "Chief wants me to get outside help and I thought of you."

Smiling, Sara turned her attention to Dagger and said, "Mick."

"Mick?" Padre asked.

With a wave of his hand, Dagger said, "The less you know, the better."

"Fine with me. Just stop by some time tonight when it's less crowded and do what ya gotta do." Padre then told them about the homicide this morning.

"She was a cop?" Sara asked.

Padre nodded. "Really bizarre. She was wedged between the branches about twenty feet up in the air. Gun was still in her holster, safety on."

Dagger's eyebrows hunched in thought. "Any suspects? What about the boyfriend?"

"Looks clean to me. We're going to focus now on any collars she's put away, someone recently released with vengeance on his brain."

"Miss me?" Sheila was all smiles as she returned from the restroom.

"Nah, we're done." Padre's gaze swept the room, force

of habit. "Who you having lunch with?"

Sheila nodded to a table by the window. "My new assistant, Caroline."

A frail looking young woman with mousy brown hair and a cocoa-brown suit, sat perusing the menu and checking her watch.

"Guess I should go eat." She gave Dagger a quick peck on the cheek and to Padre she said, "Nice seeing you." Again, she said nothing to Sara.

"Probably college age," Padre said about the mousy looking assistant. "Dulls herself up so she doesn't shine in front of her boss but all the while gleaning tips and ways to get her job."

"Probably right." Dagger watched Sheila take her seat at the table.

"I'll give her five seconds to check her purse." Padre smiled as Sheila unlatched her purse and slid her hand inside, leaned across the table toward her assistant, smiling in victory. "Come to papa, now."

They watched as Sheila placed her hand to her ear, the tiny recorder hidden in her grasp.

"Oh, yeah. Hope the acoustics in this place are good." Padre chuckled, shaking his head.

The look of triumph on Sheila's face slowly faded as she listened to Padre's recording. Her head turned sharply. Padre smiled broadly and raised a hand, fingers wiggling like a parent waving at a toddler.

"Damn, I hate reporters," Padre grumbled.

6

October 9, 1:20 p.m.

"How are you feeling?"

The young woman's eyes opened and she smiled. "I just had a wonderful dream."

"Really?" He sat down on the bed next to her. The scent of the afternoon rain swept in through the opened window of the two-bedroom home they rented. It had been built in the 1950s and still had a coal bin down in the basement and a creaky attic above.

She rubbed her hands across her stomach. "I dreamed we were hiking through a beautiful forest. It had blossoming trees and a huge waterfall." Her eyes blinked groggily.

He kissed her forehead, then her lips. "One day soon. The doctor says you just have to stay in bed for a little while longer."

Josie had always been shy, that was one of the qualities that had attracted Brian. Very unassuming, a patch of freckles across her nose and cheeks, chin length brown hair that had a sheen to it. They had met on the Internet in a singles chat room. Her entire family had been killed in a plane crash, as was his, so he told her. Neither had any relatives. Alone in the world, two lost souls. She had been putty in his hands.

And that was good because she never questioned the erratic hours he worked or how he made his money. She never got nosy or wandered into his locked workroom downstairs where he kept all the weapons he had stolen from various police departments.

He hated to sweat so he didn't have a weightlifter's build but Josie had thought he looked like some soap actor. Josie knew she was damn lucky to have someone like Brian and was more than willing to do whatever he wanted to satisfy his needs.

"Want something to eat?" He brushed her hair from her face. "How about a grilled cheese? Lots of protein."

She smiled and shoved herself to a sitting position. "Want help?"

"You stay." He flashed a dimpled smile and kissed her again.

Brian moved to the kitchen which the owners had upgraded. Before and after pictures had been left in the cabinet above the counter as proof, Brian thought, as to why they were charging $750 a month rent. It was a dump, but living in the ritzy part of town would be too high profile.

He grabbed the package off the butcher-block kitchen table and made his way down the creaking stairs to the basement. Decades-old watermarks stained the battleship gray-painted walls contributing to the musty odor. Nothing would erase the smell. The house was just too damn old. The foundation had seeped over the years and patchwork attempts could be seen in the corners. The washer and dryer were set on concrete stands one foot off the floor. Clotheslines hugged the low ceiling as reminders of pre-automatic dryer years.

The only thing new in the basement was the padlock Brian had placed on the door, not that he didn't trust Josie. He just knew human nature and soon she would be curious. The workroom was the old coal bin and it had taken Brian two months to clean it up and air it out. The house was now heated by a gas furnace, so there was no need for the bin or the duct that led to the furnace room. The duct had been blocked off on the other side.

Brian opened the envelope, took out the stacks of bills and shoved them into their hiding place in the unused duct. The only piece of furniture in the ten-foot-by-fifteen-foot room was a twin-sized bed shoved against the wall. He sat down and contemplated his next move. If only he could get his hands on the cache of weapons confiscated last night. But those wouldn't be in the Evidence Room. ATF probably had them by now. Doesn't matter, he thought, because he had seen several Heckler & Koch UMP45 submachine guns during his last visit to the room. Those alone should net him a pretty penny.

Checking his watch, he locked the room and returned to the kitchen to make Josie something to eat.

* * *

By the time Padre reached J.D.'s townhouse, the light drizzle had just started to let up and the sun was making a bold attempt to burn through the overcast skies. He watched a woman hurry out of the car in front of him and cross the street to the same townhouse. She was carrying a black bag and all kinds of thoughts started running through Padre's head. Mainly, did a guilty J.D. attempt to commit suicide?

Padre hurried out of his car and reached the front door just as J.D. opened it.

"This way," J.D. told them. He made quick introductions as he led them through a living room with a vaulted ceiling, down a hall, through the compact kitchen and out the back door.

The gray-haired, agile woman with the black bag was Doctor Dorothy Abrams, a veterinarian. Square-framed glasses hung from a beaded chain around her neck.

"I found him when I came home. Scared the hell out of me. You'll see why." J.D. led them through the patio, around to the back of the two-car garage. There, cowering under the burnt orange spirea was Max. His fur was matted, body shaking.

"Oh, my poor Max," Doctor Abrams gasped.

"Wait, I need an evidence bag," Padre said.

"I have some," Doctor Abrams replied.

"Lisa bought Max from Doc Abrams," J.D. explained. "When I found him I thought he might respond better to her. I didn't want to approach him and risk contaminating any evidence he might have on him. He might have scratched the killer."

"That's good." Padre studied the lolling head of the Doberman, the vacant eyes, the ragged breathing.

"And I wanted Doc Abrams here in case he had something serious wrong with him."

She opened her case, pulled out brown paper evidence bags and handed them to Padre, then slipped into latex gloves. Staying close to the ground she made a move toward the shivering dog.

"Hey, Max. Sweetie. Grandma DoDo's here and everything is going to be fine." Getting up close, she held her arm out but he didn't sniff her. "I'm only going to check you out, Max. Can you stay still for me?" The Doberman didn't seem to acknowledge her presence.

Doc Abrams said, "He's got glassy eyes, seems disoriented." Cautiously, she touched his jaw. "It's okay. Let me check your gums, Sweetie." She patted his head, got up closer, felt his body tremble. "He's in shock. Gums are pale, he's weak. J.D., I need you to go get some honey or karo syrup and warm water. I'm going to give him some benadryl." She gave a cursory glance toward Padre. "Sergeant, he'll be still for you if you want to bag his paws. I'll scrape them when I get him back to the clinic." She filled a hypodermic and gave Max an injection. "I'm going to have to keep him a couple days. We need to get an I.V. in him."

Padre bent down and helped band the bags on the Doberman's paws. "Aren't Dobermans supposed to be great guard dogs?"

"I trained Max myself," she replied stroking the dogs trembling body. "He would sooner rip a guy's head off than let any harm come to Lisa."

"What could do this?"

"Not sure."

"Stun gun? Mega dose of electricity?"

Her hand paused over the dog's chest. "I don't think so. This dog has literally been scared to death."

7

October 9, 6:05 p.m.

Dagger slipped another coin into the vending machine and pressed a button. A can clanged through the chute and rolled down to the receptacle. He peered toward the door at the end of the hall as he retrieved his Pepsi. It was a little after six o'clock, three hours since the changing of the crews. There was something eerie about being in the bowels of Headquarters. Hallways branched like a maze, leading toward the garage, a storage room for archived files, and a supply room.

He tried to visualize in his mind how someone could gain access to the scanner and leave without anyone seeing him. Even if an outsider gained access through the garage, he still wouldn't get past the scanner. Had to be Riley. But wouldn't someone have recognized a fellow cop who had retired? Wouldn't they have said, "Hey, Louie, how's the retirement going?" Or, "I hear you're having the life of Riley," seeing that his last name was Riley.

Padre hadn't talked much about the homicide. Whenever there was a case involving a fellow cop, Padre kept quiet, as if a close family member had died. But basically it was family, to him. He had told Dagger about the condition of the victim's dog and how he had a staff researching the case history of Officer Cambridge. Unfortunately, or fortunately, Lisa hadn't been a cop long enough to make that many enemies. Dagger hadn't pressured him.

The door at the end of the hall opened and Padre waved him over. "All clear." Padre led him past an empty desk. "This is where the clerk used to sit." Then he showed him the wall by the door. He pressed START on a keypad, then inserted his index finger into a slot no bigger than a change return. A green light flickered and a buzzer sounded.

As they passed through the doorway, Padre explained, "Guess these biometrics are a new fad. They are going to start to install them in cars. No longer need a key. Thieves won't be able to steal your car. They are even thinking of putting the chips on credit cards."

"Skizzy would have fun with that. Big Brother is always watching."

"Got that right."

The Evidence Room contained movable shelving units reaching up to a twelve-foot-tall ceiling. It resembled an old time library with shelves built into the walls and a rollaway ladder. File boxes sat side by side on the shelves.

Padre pointed to the numbers written on the boxes. "Everything is in numerical order by case number so you aren't going to find all the weapons in one spot." He looked Dagger over as if sizing him up. "Where's all your gear?"

Dagger patted the pockets of his vest. "Got everything I need right here."

With a shake of his head Padre left him and went to stand guard.

Skizzy checked the clock above the door of his pawn shop. His bulging eyes shifted back and forth as if he were mentally clicking off the seconds.

"I don't think it's against the law to close early. Right?" Sara studied Dagger's friend. His gray hair was short in spots, as if he had ripped out sections in a paranoid frenzy. The rest was long and worn mostly in a ponytail.

"Law?" He jerked his head toward her. "Laws are the government's way of keeping us in line, taking away our freedoms." His gaze snapped back to the clock, then his wristwatch. "My watch is forty-five seconds off. I missed forty-five seconds somewhere, probably abducted. But I was able to free myself. This time." He splayed open the blinds on the small pane of window in the door and peered outside. "Maybe not next time." The blinds snapped shut. "Gotta be on your guard."

Sara winced as Skizzy worked his way down the door frame, bolting all seven locks then slamming the steel brace across the door. She didn't know why he bothered. He'll have to undo them all when she leaves.

"Dagger said six-fifteen," she reminded him.

"Let's get a move on then."

He led her through the curtained doorway to his back room where he pressed a button on the bookcase. It slid open and they made their way down the steep staircase to the paneled basement. Fluorescent bulbs overhead brightened the makeshift bomb shelter with its shelves of bottled water and canned goods.

Three monitors on the table glowed, surrounded by a multitude of immobile Micks. Sara eagerly sat down and picked up one of the bugs, set it in the palm of her hand.

"These are a masterpiece. You are brilliant."

"Why, thank you, little lady." He flitted around the room like a drone bee from the filing cabinet to a shelf and back to the table. "But Dagger is really the brains behind it."

"Testing." Dagger's voice came over the speaker. "Anyone there?"

The monitors came alive showing three different views of the evidence room at headquarters. Skizzy punched a few buttons and four views appeared on screen.

"Loud and clear," Skizzy reported.

Dagger tapped his ear piece. He was standing on a ladder in front of one of the Micks he had placed on a narrow ledge above the shelving.

"What keeps it from falling?" Sara asked.

"Magnet," Skizzy replied. "Dagger has it right on top of a nail head."

"Make sure this one catches the entrance," Dagger said. "I want you to be able to get a full length view."

"Then you're going to have to move it further back. And unless Mick is outside of the room across from the scanner, it ain't gonna pick up squat."

"Can't do that. There isn't anything to attach it to except the wall. And someone will knock it down in no time."

"Then we'll have to settle for seeing his face and his hand. Best we can do."

Dagger stood in the doorway, waving his hands at the camera.

"Yeah, yeah, we see you. Now where is the next one going?"

"Camera two," Dagger said as he pulled out his remote and pressed a button. Another Mick was moving across the top of a cabinet, which was bolted to the wall. "If they ever decide to remove these cabinets, we are going to be in big trouble."

"Only if they can trace it," Skizzy said.

Sara asked, "Can they?"

"If they are smarter than us." Dagger's waving hands could be seen in the second screen. In less than fifteen minutes he had placed four Micks which easily monitored the majority of the room. He didn't want too many in case he had to come back and quickly remove them.

"You know, we should put one in every politician's office. Maybe the Oval Office." Skizzy chuckled and started to do what he did best—talk to himself. "We'll get them. Catch them in their lies and deceit. The FBI, CIA. Keep tabs on them like they keep tabs on us."

Sara slowly shifted her gaze from the screen to Skizzy. His pupils seemed dilated, eyes wide, like a mad scientist mulling over the results of an experiment. She felt sorry for him sitting there in a stained tee shirt and camouflage pants, mumbling to himself as if he had spent half his life in a prison camp and was just let out into the real world.

"It's probably a government man used the scanner,

testing out some government invention to duplicate our fingerprints."

Dagger's unshaven face and intense eyes glared on the monitor. "What the hell are you mumbling about, Skizzy?"

"Government boys. They are the ones probably found a way to duplicate our prints."

Dagger lifted his gaze toward the ceiling in disbelief at another one of his friend's conspiracy theories.

Sara watched Skizzy start to rock back and forth, mumbling, his hands still playing with the keyboard.

"They had something like that in a movie," she offered. "In *Demolition Man* they had a retina scanner. Wesley Snipe's character plucked the eye out of a dead guy and used it to gain clearance through the scanner."

Dagger turned back to the monitor, his eyebrows inching upward. "What?"

Skizzy finally stopped rocking and stared at her. He then said something that sounded incredulous especially coming from him. "Girl, you are watching way too much television."

8

October 9, 8:05 p.m.

Padre turned away from the window and contemplated his umteenth cup of coffee. Lately, coffee seemed to be his only choice of sustenance. He dropped down in a chair behind the table and peered through the glass at the autopsy room.

Next to telling relatives about their deceased loved ones, he detested witnessing autopsies. Padre knew it was necessary in determining cause of death but in all his years as a cop, he still considered it to be the ultimate violation of the human body. This was where reality set in. We were an elaborate network of bones and tissue and wholly dependent upon air, water, and food, not to mention the heart which pumps the nutrients to all parts of the body. Then one day someone flips the switch leaving nothing but an empty shell.

Padre sipped his coffee and found his gaze drifting back to Lisa's body. He remembered seeing her often in the gym. She could kick box the shit out of any of the guys on the

force and out-bench press half of them. J.D. had been her
trainer. They had even been on the cover of one of the
weight training magazines.

Padre looked up when Luther entered. The little guy was
wiping beads of perspiration from his dark skin. He took a
seat across from Padre. Luther had once attended mortician
school. But dressing the deceased when working part time at
a local mortuary only brought questions to his mind. Why
did this person die so young? What was the true cause of
death? It always took him longer to apply makeup to camouflage injuries because Luther would be assessing the
wound, wondering what type of weapon had been used.

It was Leon Steinholz, the seventy-year-old owner of the
mortuary who had noticed Luther's inquisitive nature. He
was the one who pointed out Luther's true passion. Leon,
with his cue ball head and pointed features, had taken Luther
to Al's Deli for matzo ball soup. Luther thought he was
going to be fired for taking twice as long as the other stu-
dents in preparing bodies. Instead, Leon had an offer that
would change Luther's life.

Mortuary school was a two-year course. Luther's parents
couldn't afford the type of education required for a career in
forensics. It was Leon who paid for Luther's schooling.

"This was a toughie," Luther said, popping open a can of
Diet Pepsi.

"Always tough when it's a cop."

"And when the victim is young." Luther rested his glasses on the table and opened the case folder. He had pointed
out to Padre during the autopsy the single deep cut-throat
lesion which had severed Lisa's carotid arteries. No multiple

wounds, no sexual contact. There hadn't even been any defense wounds on her hands.

"Any idea what I'm going to tell the chief?" Padre asked. His question was met with silence.

Padre had studied every inch of Lisa's body with Luther. The M.E. had suggested waiting until tomorrow to see if any markings appeared. But for the present, they had been unable to see any bruising or rope burns to indicate how Lisa's body ended up wedged in a forked limb twenty feet above the ground.

9

October 9, 9:58 p.m.

"So either you or Skizzy can record what's happening?"
Sara stared inquisitively at the monitor on Dagger's desk
where split screens showed what each of the Micks was
viewing. "Can you both watch at the same time?"

"We are now." Dagger bent over Sara's shoulder,
inhaled a subtle trace of citrus from her hair, and punched a
few keys. "Skizzy, can you hear me?"

"Loud and clear," the voice blared from the speakers.
"Not much action."

"Neat," Sara said, smiling. "Are they motion-activated?"

"That girl's getting too smart for us," Skizzy said.

"SMARTY SMARTY." Einstein's sturdy claws clamped
onto the perch by Dagger's desk.

"Hey. You're supposed to be asleep," Dagger told the
macaw. Turning back to the monitor, he told Skizzy, "Let me
know in the morning if there's anything worth watching."

"Will do."

Dagger switched off the computer and stretched. "Okay, Buddy." He walked over to the grated door and rattled it. "In you go."

Einstein settled down on the perch and looked away from Dagger.

"I think he's looking for a bribe." Sara opened the top desk drawer and withdrew a Brazil nut. Einstein riveted a beady eye at the treat as Sara pitched it to Dagger.

"Look what I have, Einstein." Dagger held the Brazil nut in his fingers.

Einstein's toes clamped and unclamped around the perch as if doing a little dance, not quite sure whether to stay put or go. Finally, he flew into the aviary and landed on the perch inside the doorway. He gingerly picked the nut out of Dagger's hand.

It was dark in the aviary. The lights were on a timer, and although there were blinds between the double panes on the skylights, they were closed only during thunderstorms.

Dagger slid the doors shut. He clicked on the television set and stretched out on the couch, hoping the news had the latest information on the recent homicide.

"How about some coffee?" Dagger yelled out. After a few seconds, he craned his neck to see Sara standing behind the couch, her eyes like narrow slits, arms crossed. He was sure if he peered over the back of the couch, he would see her bare toes tapping. Simon had warned Dagger before that he should appreciate Sara more, that Dagger sometimes treated her like a lap dog, fetching things for him without so much as a thank you in return. At first, Sara bent over backwards to please him, fearful she might otherwise have no one to protect her. "Please," he finally added.

"That's better."

He watched her leave, smiling at how much better his shirts looked on her. Although she rolled the sleeves up, the shirttails touched the backs of her knees. They looked great over her leggings. But what he loved most was grabbing the shirts after she wore them, inhaling her perfume or the smell of her hair, residues that clung to the fabric.

"You are one sick puppy," he whispered to himself just as the buzzer on the front gate pierced the air.

Shutters on the pass-through behind the bar were pushed open and Sara peered out to make sure Dagger was answering the intercom.

The faces of two men appeared on the monitor. The driver of the dark sedan was scraggly, tie eschew, shirt wrinkled. His eyes were puffy and he was sipping on a cup through a plastic lid. The man next to him was younger, elbow propped on the door frame, fist pressed wearily to his chin.

"You Chase Dagger?" The driver asked.

"Who wants to know?" Dagger barked.

"I'm Sergeant Marty Flynn with the Indianapolis P.D." He gave a nod toward his passenger. "This here's Professor William Sherlock of Purdue University. Padre said we should talk to you."

Dagger chuckled at the name. "How do you know Padre?" Dagger could read lips halfway decent and *shit* just crossed the older man's lips. "Hang on a minute." *Shit* just crossed Dagger's lips as he grabbed his cellular and called Padre. Padre would never tell anyone where he lived without running it past him first.

"Padre," Dagger said when the cop answered the phone. "Forget to tell me something?"

Shit crossed Padre's lips and he explained, "I know, I'm sorry. Shoulda' called but I've really been busy and when Marty stopped by with this theory of his I just knew there was no way I could let him loose in this precinct much less in this town with that viper of a reporter we have lurking. What he has to say is right up your alley."

Dagger stared at his cellular after hanging up. A little voice in his head said if he let these guys in he was going to regret it. But his thumb pressed the OPEN button and he watched on the monitor as the gate swung free. It closed as the dark sedan lumbered through.

The professor was much taller than Dagger had expected. The image on the monitor had appeared smaller in frame. He still wasn't quite as tall as Dagger and he had strange-looking streaks of white running through his hair. Wire-rimmed glasses befitting a scholarly professor rested on his nose.

Sergeant Flynn gave new meaning to the word disheveled. If they were staying in a hotel, they obviously hadn't checked in yet. His trench coat barely survived the ride from Indianapolis, the back all bunched and wrinkled. It was difficult to tell that they had ridden together since the professor looked wrinkle-free, as though he had stood up during the entire trip.

The sergeant gave a quick cop's once-over at Dagger's appearance, his gaze sweeping the length of Dagger's tall frame and settling on the ponytail, the diamond-studded earring, the wolf head pendant hanging from a leather cord around his neck, and the clothes better served on nighttime reconnaissance. They exchanged niceties and Marty explained that he and Padre had met at a one-month FBI training session at Quantico several years ago. They stripped out of their coats and Dagger tossed them on the backs of the barstools.

Marty and Dagger sat at opposite ends of the couch. Professor Sherlock laid claim to the loveseat and cocktail table, opening up his laptop, and spreading papers next to it.

"Padre said you had a theory about the murder this morning?" Dagger said.

"We've been tracking a killer, or I should say, I've been tracking a killer since March of ninety-eight," the sergeant replied. Sherlock here," he tossed a quick nod toward the professor, "has been tracking him much longer."

"Same guy?" Dagger leaned back into the corner of the couch, curiously watching Sherlock jam a disk into the computer.

"Not exactly," Sherlock said.

"We had a string of murders in Indianapolis in ninety-eight. They were brutal, escalating by the hour. Thought it was a damn mountain lion escaped from the Indianapolis zoo." Marty looked over his shoulder toward the bar.

"I have coffee brewing now," Dagger said, "but I can get you something stronger."

Marty's hand swiped across his mouth, like an alcoholic salivating for his next drink. "I'd love it but unfortunately we have to keep a clear head. We don't have much time."

Dagger caught Sherlock checking the clock on the wall

by the desk. The professor was jumpy. Hell, they both were jumpy. Padre probably hurled these two at him just to get them out of his hair.

"Little more than three days. That's all we have left." Sherlock went back to the laptop. Click, click. His long fingers flew over the keyboard.

"Three days?" Dagger had just about all he could take of this cryptic dialogue. "Okay. Exactly what happens in three days?"

Sherlock looked up from his keyboard. "Have you ever heard of a shape-shifter?"

A loud crash reverberated near the door to the aviary. Sara stood, her arms raised as if her fingers still clutched the serving tray. On the quarry tile in front of her were broken cups, saucers, and carafe, the shards lying in a pool of coffee.

Dagger ran to her aid and grabbed her arms. Her eyes were unblinking as she stared at Sherlock. Dagger's voice was low and he had to force a smile, still trying to digest what Sherlock had said. "Sara, look at me." Finally, she tore her gaze from their guests. "Sara, I want you to go upstairs and put some shoes on. I'll clean this up. Go."

Marty helped by placing the broken cups and carafe on the tray and carrying them to the kitchen. By the time Sara returned, Dagger had mopped up the floor, pulled back the area rug so it could dry, and brought out more coffee and cups.

Sara wanted to hide in the kitchen where she could eavesdrop, but then the professor said, "You're Native American, aren't you?"

Sara nodded and looked to Dagger for direction. He motioned to the chair next to him as he explained to the two men, "Sara Morningsky is my assistant." He watched as the two men looked from Sara to the surroundings. Dagger was getting tired of explaining his and Sara's living and working arrangements. Even when he went through the legitimate explanation that he rented office and living space from Sara and that they had a business relationship, people would look at him with a "who are you trying to kid?" expression on their faces. So he just gave up trying.

Sherlock told Sara, "I guess what I said frightened you. Can we ask you some questions?"

"I just hadn't heard the term in a long time," Sara replied as she slid onto the chair, tucking her legs under her. She accepted the cup of coffee Dagger had poured for her.

Sherlock sifted through his notes and continued. "Members of the Lewis and Clark Expedition have entries in their diaries referring to what their Indian guides called a beast-man, or *manitou*. These manitous supposedly could change themselves into wolves."

Sara's hands shook as she brought the cup to her mouth. Dagger's piercing gaze was a gesture of warning. She willed her hands to stop shaking, set the cup down and clasped her hands in her lap.

"We just thought of them as fairy tales, like your people would tell ghost stories. We never thought it was something real," Sara explained.

Dagger leaned forward, elbows on his knees. "Wait a second, gentlemen. You're going to tell me the cop this morning was killed by some guy who changed into a wolf and ripped her throat out? I take it you haven't read the report. She was found twenty feet above the ground in a tree." He walked over to the bar and poured scotch into a glass of ice and added a splash of water.

Marty explained, "The damn thing can change into a bird."

Sara jerked her gaze back to Dagger as he returned to the couch. Her hands started trembling again and one knuckle found its way to her mouth as she started to nibble frantically on it.

Marty stared at the liquor saying, "Just want you to know, you are really going to need your wits about you."

"I think real good on a shot of scotch." Dagger took a swallow and winced, chased it with a sip of coffee. "Let me see if I have this straight. We need to find an Indian who is changing into a wolf and…" he looked at the two men finding it difficult to keep the smile from spreading across his face, "what kind of bird?"

"Anything he wants." Sherlock stopped typing and gathered up some papers. "But he isn't Native American. And he can't change at will. Only when there is a full moon. And that will be in a little more than three days. Three-fifty-four on Friday morning to be exact."

"And he's particularly brutal when it falls on a Friday the thirteenth," Marty added.

"So now we're looking for a modern day wolf man." Dagger chuckled, leaned back against the cushions and stared up at the catwalk. With a shake of his head, he said, "Remind me to thank Padre for this one."

10

October 9, 11:15 p.m.

"You better start at the beginning." Dagger set his empty glass aside, wondering how soon he could get rid of these two nut cases. He refilled his coffee cup and glanced quickly at Sara, her young eyes wide, like a startled deer.

Sherlock rubbed his eyes and shoved the sleeves up on his cable knit sweater. There was a slight tremble in his fingers as he reached for a stack of papers. He gulped his coffee, a substance Dagger had a feeling he had been living on for far too long. Over the rim of his cup, Sherlock's gaze took in his surroundings, as if assessing the safety of the house.

"I witnessed the murder of my family when I was six years old," Sherlock started. "My brother, Joey, who was twelve, was babysitting me." He took his time, staring vacantly as if seeing the entire scene replaying in his mind. "My brother and I were playing hide-and-seek when my parents came home. My mother thought they had been fol-

lowed. I could hear the fear in her voice. Before I could
come out of my hiding place, someone…something broke
down the door."

Dagger studied Sara who seemed captivated by the
story, as if she were still the child listening to scary stories
told by the elders.

"I was hiding in a toy box about the size of a small hope
chest. The sides were made of some kind of sturdy peg-
board. It had small holes in it but I could still see." Sherlock
glanced over at Dagger. "I say something because it
changed. It was a man and then it was this animal, wolf I
think, but it walked upright."

Dagger's gaze shifted from Sherlock to Sergeant Flynn.
The cop was the image of a man ready for retirement. There
was grease under his nails and Dagger guessed he was a car
buff who did his own repairs and oil changes. His shoes
were polished which clashed with the wrinkled attire so
Dagger guessed him to be married to an adoring wife who
made sure her husband's suits were cleaned and shoes polished. It was what the sergeant did to the clothes once they
were on his body that told Dagger volumes.

Sergeant Flynn was someone who was more interested
in his cases than his appearance. Professor Sherlock had
handed him a puzzling case in ninety-eight and the sergeant
just couldn't retire until he had it solved.

But the sergeant also seemed to have his head on
straight, not chase outrageous theories. So why travel three
hours chasing something completely preposterous? And
why wasn't Dagger throwing them both out? Why was he
sucking it all up, engrossed as much as Sara? Maybe he had

been hanging around Skizzy too much. Or maybe he had been living with Sara too long.

Finally, Dagger asked, "Professor, exactly what do you teach at Purdue?"

"Astronomy and Human Behavior."

"Astronomy? Not Astrology?"

"That, too, somewhat."

Dagger chuckled.

"He's had those streaks of white in his hair since he was six years old. Now will you let him finish his story?" Marty barked, brushing a hand across the damp hair clinging to his forehead.

"I was in shock for several weeks," Sherlock continued. "Didn't remember anything for the longest time. Then I started to have nightmares in my early twenties. Large wolves who walked on their hind legs, predators with razor-sharp teeth changing into winged monsters."

"Let me guess, repressed memories." Dagger's comment brought another sharp glare from Marty.

Sherlock stared at his computer screen, clasped his hands together until the fingers started to turn white. He looked over at Sara, then to Dagger. "My family died on November 13, 1970. A Friday and a full moon. Ten years ago I started researching similar occurrences. My research took me to Philadelphia, Trenton, Rochester. Naturally, police records were incomplete. If there were any eyewitnesses, they are dead. After all, we're talking about the year 1919 and earlier."

"Wait," Dagger uncrossed his legs, sat up, his eyes curiously drawn to the stacks of papers. "I thought you said the killings were current?"

"There have been twelve instances of a full moon on a Friday the thirteenth since 1800. I had run into a brick wall, given up. Until the murders at Purdue in 1987. I called with only one important question. I asked if the victims' watches had stopped at one-twenty-eight in the morning. I ended up being dragged in as a suspect."

Dagger would definitely have to call Padre and thank him for dumping these two guys on his doorstep. No wonder Padre didn't have time for this. No wonder he didn't want the press to catch wind of Sherlock's theory.

"The watches HAD stopped at that exact time," Marty chimed in.

"How did you hook up with the professor, Sergeant?"

"Back in 1998, week of March 9, we had a number of brutal killings. Claw marks, bodies ripped apart."

"I thought you said it was specifically on the thirteenth?" Dagger could feel himself being pulled in. The only way to keep them from talking was to keep from asking questions. But he just hadn't learned when to shut up.

Sherlock said, "There are several killings during normal full moons. I believe he remains in human form. Can't shift until the combination of a full moon on a Friday the thirteenth. Then, during those rare occasions, the murders escalate leading up to the thirteenth, as the killer is becoming more creature and his thirst for destruction more intense. And right after the official full moon, it stops."

"In Indianapolis," Marty continued, "a woman had her throat slashed, claw marks left on the back of the seat. Then a bus driver, ripped stem to sternum. Scratch marks on the back of the bus."

"Could have been a hoax. Something to throw you off. And a wound from talons would have left more than one cut wound," Dagger said.

"He thinks like a human," Sherlock said. "Use one talon, let the authorities think it's a human. Throw them off track. He's very cunning."

"Just as the professor said," Marty further explained, "the closer it got to the exact time of the full moon in 1998, the more brutal the attacks. Wiped out a cleaning crew working the late shift at a local fast food joint."

"Anyone check a local zoo?"

Marty grabbed some of the papers from one of the stacks and handed them to Dagger. "Yep, did that. All the large animals were accounted for."

Dagger stared at glossy eight-by-tens of each of the victims. The first two could have been killed by any number of weapons. But it was the last picture of the three bodies in the cooler at the fast food restaurant that got to him. It was as though someone had taken a fabric doll they no longer wanted and ripped it to shreds. Body parts had been strewn about, like parts of that doll. But unfortunately, these couldn't be sewn back together.

Marty pointed at the last picture. An African American woman, eyes wide in horror, slash marks across her body. "Chiffon also cleaned one of the schools. Nice lady. Just before she died she told me she saw IT." Marty stared at Dagger, wanting to make sure he had heard him. "She said IT changed into a bird and flew away."

Click, click. Sherlock's fingers started to dance on the

keyboard. Dagger glanced again at Sara. Her eyes like huge blue orbs. She had remained silent throughout the entire story. Her body never flinched. So it surprised Dagger when she finally spoke.

"Can it regenerate?" Sara asked, her voice barely audible above the clicking of the keys.

Sherlock peered up, surprise on his face, a look reserved for prize pupils who easily understood his theories. "Why, yes. And it can only be killed in human form."

Sara reached for the pictures in Dagger's lap. "May I?"

"I don't think you want..." Dagger saw the determination on her face. She kept her hand outstretched until he handed them to her.

Sara swallowed hard and winced at the crime scene. She thumbed through them slowly, hoping there was some other explanation. When she came across a picture of what looked like a littered floor, she held it up. "What's this?"

Marty leaned forward. "The techs found fur and feathers at the crime scene. Both were from unknown species. Definitely not synthetic." The cop stared intently at Dagger, as if making sure he had his total attention. "All of the victim's watches had stopped the exact time of the full moon on March thirteenth. They wouldn't have found identical samples at your morning crime scene, Mr. Dagger. But check again on the thirteenth."

Dagger felt a knot slowly creep up his spine, like a foreign object seeking a way out. The last thing he needed was to find an ounce of truth in what they were saying. He didn't want to believe, couldn't believe. But there was something in their voices. Call it fear, conviction, whatever. He tried to keep some logic in his thinking.

"You seem to have gone through a lot of research, Professor." Dagger stared at the stacks of file folders, the reams of reports. "But I'm sure you have heard of Big Foot, the Loch Ness Monster, the Abominable Snowman, all just rumored sightings with no concrete evidence."

"There are many things in life we can't explain. But one thing is certain...I know what I saw." The professor held up the crime scene photos from two years ago. "And this should be proof enough that there is a vicious killer out there."

Dagger glanced at Sara and held her gaze. A year ago no one would have convinced him shape-shifters existed. Then he met Sara. But she was an anomaly, a one-of-a-kind. He can only deal with one anomaly in his lifetime.

To Sherlock, he said, "I thought it didn't shift totally until the day of the full moon."

Sherlock pushed the laptop away, checked the clock on the wall again. "It's the degree of shifting and how long he maintains it that I believe is controlled by the energy from the full moon. I mentioned we have had twelve full moons on a Friday the thirteenth since 1800. This will be the thirteenth one. I believe he will be more powerful than he has ever been. And with each generation, the evil is becoming even stronger."

"Generation?" Sara unfolded her legs and felt a shudder reverberate through her body. "What do you mean?"

Sherlock passed additional reports to Dagger, saying, "The killer's name is Paul Addison. Every male in the Addison family born on a Friday the thirteenth has had this shifting ability. There has been one every generation. They seem to have a pecking order. When one dies, the next in line seems to immediately take on this ability."

Dagger stared at the Addison Family Tree Sherlock had drawn:

Paul, November 13, 1970
Trent, February 14, 1930
Cleveland, October 13, 1905
Seymour, May 13, 1881
Henry, June 13, 1851
Nathan, February 13, 1835

Sherlock explained, "You will notice Paul's father, Trent, wasn't born on a Friday the thirteenth. It was Trent's father, Cleveland, who raped Paul's mother. Cleveland was Paul's father."

Dagger digested that information, the professor's credibility was fading the more information he dispelled. "Nathan was only sixteen when he fathered a son?"

Sherlock replied, "Yes."

"Why them?" Dagger asked. "Why the Addison family and no one else?"

With a heavy sigh and a rake of fingers through his streaked hair, Sherlock admitted, "I'm not sure at this point. But according to some old newspaper accounts and town rumors, Nathan Addison was a witch. Not the traditional wiccan of today which certainly doesn't call for casting spells and conjuring up the devil. He delved into the unknown, robbed gravesites, conducted human sacrifices. He was a strange kid and claimed he was rewarded for coming to the dark side, whatever the hell that means."

* * *

Sara stretched out on the window seat in her room staring at the sky. In the early hours of Friday morning the moon would be full. What if everything their visitors said were true? Was there really someone else out there like her? If her grandmother were still alive, she would have the answers...maybe.

A shadow filled her doorway and she heard a knock on the door frame. "Are you okay?" Dagger crossed the room and sat across from her.

Sara gathered her robe around her to ward off the chill penetrating her bones. Dagger placed his hands on her ankles. His skin was warm, almost hot to the touch. She stared at him in her darkened room, light from the moon slicing a pattern across his face. His eyes were intense as he tightened his grip. There was something reassuring in his gaze, in his touch. She trusted him completely, with her life, with her safety.

"Do you believe them, Dagger?"

He released his grip and leaned back, eyes staring at the large ball of light in the sky, which bathed the acres in a soft glow.

She followed his gaze and said with resignation, "There might be someone out there just like me."

"No." He shook his head and the shadows made his eyes appear more feral. "The way this guy kills, you can't possibly make the comparison."

"The wolf can be just as deadly, kill just as ferociously." She looked away from him, back to the sky. According to

Indian mythology, there can be no witnesses to a shifting. Sara's wolf form would kill any witnesses and it was something she couldn't control. So her grandparents had moved her around the country to get Sara as far away as possible so the wolf wouldn't be tempted.

"You heard the professor, Sara. This is different. He only shifts during a full moon on a Friday the thirteenth. You know, werewolves and..." Dagger shook his head and chuckled. "God, listen to me. I'm talking like I believe them." He pressed his head against the wall and sighed. His eyes revealed the fatigue settling over his body. "My gut tells me the killer is a very sick, perverted serial killer. Someone who knows how to yank someone's chain. He's cunning, sinister, and enjoys watching the authorities chase around like Keystone Cops. But he's human, Sara."

"Still..." They were silent for a while, each studying the clear sky and the moon looming over the treetops. Slowly, Sara shifted her gaze back to Dagger's face, the handsome, angular features, the scar above his left eyebrow, the result of a recent case they had worked on. "I have to find out for sure, Dagger." She whispered it as though the air might carry her words through the opened patio door to whatever lie in waiting outside.

Sara rose from the window seat and walked toward the patio door, slid open the screen. Returning, she tossed her robe on the bed. With one last gaze at Dagger, she shifted into the gray wolf. The change was swift, one fluid motion. And she was becoming more comfortable each time shifting in front of him.

He never saw even a hint of bare skin. It always amazed

him. For some reason *Beam me up Scotty* always ran through his head when he watched. One second Sara was standing there in all her innocent beauty, and then her five-foot-six-inch frame seemed to diminish, her features combine briefly with the wolf, and then the wolf materialized. The only feature that didn't change were those mesmerizing eyes. Even the nightgown seemed to drift from her body and now lay pooled at the wolf's paws.

Each time he told himself to watch carefully but there was too much to focus on in trying to watch the face, skin, legs, hoping to witness the entire process. He never succeeded. The change was just too quick.

The wolf kept its distance, as fearful of him as Sara had once been. But it would never harm him. Dagger was Sara's protector. He had saved the wolf once, and Sara's grandmother had given him the black cord necklace with the silver wolf head pendant which had turquoise stones embedded for eyes.

The wolf took two timid steps backward, turned, bounded out onto the balcony and just as quickly, shifted to the gray hawk as it landed on the railing.

Be careful, Sara.

11

Tuesday, October 10, 12:20 a.m.

Tex secretly smiled as he turned off Route 12 onto Camden Parkway. His baby was two days old and now he would be able to see what she could do. His baby was his new Harley motorcycle, the Fat Boy®. Tex had saved for five years to outfit his baby to his dream bike. Twenty-one thousand dollars it cost and he had never in his life felt such power between his legs. Six hundred and ninety-five pounds of sheer energy.

The eight inch headlamp revealed an open stretch of road ahead, the perfect place to let her out, see what she could do. Tex turned the volume up so the whole world could hear LeAnn Rimes' sweet voice on his premium sound system. Tex had his own band, Tex's Rangers. They played mostly red-neck bars and county fairs. And he was always amused at the surprise on the faces in the audience when he pulled his two-hundred-and-forty-pound body onto the stage carrying a delicate fiddle. People expected him to be carrying some monstrous ass instrument or to be pounding on a drum. But his granddaddy had taught him how to play the fiddle and somehow his fat stubby fingers were able to make those strings sing.

Tex watched the speedometer register seventy-five, eight, ninety, as the wind played through his hair and the forest swallowed him up. This was a stretch of road seldom used, except for the occasional high school hot rodders. Insects ricocheted off the windshield and he was thankful he had remembered to bring his protective glasses.

He opened her up and the Fat Boy® took the curve with ease, a throaty roar of the engine echoing through the night air. Something darted across the road ahead and Tex switched on the high beam. Last thing he needed was to impale a deer on the front of his new toy.

Brightly colored leaves drifted across the road. The high beam cast shadows in the thick underbrush beyond the grassy shoulders lining Camden Parkway. Thick limbs reached far enough across the road to touch its neighbors.

The road dipped and an eerie mist curled around the trees and snaked across his path. There was a damp chill to the air, which penetrated Tex's leather jacket. It felt as though the temperature had just dropped twenty degrees.

Tex didn't have a care in the world. His dream had come true. Let the rich cats have their Cadillacs and Lincolns. He had his Fat Boy®, although his wife would argue he could have bought a car with the price he paid for his dream.

He was in the middle of these happy thoughts when the pain hit him. The burning spread across his neck and down his chest and he vaguely remembered a face looming in front of him, coming from nowhere. It had the strangest eyes, yellow and slitted, like some wild cat. Was he suffering from the road hypnosis people feel after staring at the center line too long? He hadn't had anything to drink and definitely didn't smoke a joint before climbing on his baby.

He marveled at the chrome pipes on his Fat Boy® and how the two-tone sinister blue and diamond ice color shone under the moonlight. How absolutely beautiful his baby looked as it sailed off the road and onto the shoulder, along with the rest of his body.

He basked in the moonlight, stretched out on a thick limb of an ancient oak tree. The energy permeated every pour and he drank it in, felt himself changing. Just as much outside as inside. The lust of the kill, the hunger to destroy. So many victims, so little time. He laughed, an hysterical laugh that echoed through the forest preserve, carried on the cool winds. Wildlife scurried at the sound. Weak. All other life forms, including man, were so weak.

Nighttime rejuvenated him. He hated to sleep and understood why some writer once called sleep "little slices of death." All of his senses were enhanced. When he had first heard the droning of the motorcycle, it had sounded like a throng of bees gathering over the ridge. But there was something else. Beating...ba bump, ba bump. He could hear the sound of someone's heart. The thrill of the hunt was seductive. Ba bump, ba bump, ba bump.

His agility amazed even him. The tree limb he was reclining on was ten feet above the ground. It was barely a slight jump for him, his body propelled by some boundless energy and power. Power. He so loved that word. Power over everything and everyone. A normal full moon gave him some power and energy. Sometimes he acted on it, sometimes he didn't. And the killings read like any homicide—strangulation, blunt trauma, stabbing. All added to the list of unsolved cases over the years. And for those cases authorities claimed were solved, only he knew they had arrested the wrong man.

But it was only when the full moon occurred on a Friday the thirteenth that the insatiable craving to destroy dominated every cell of his being. The power was so intoxicating that he could think of nothing else. Soon. He could barely contain himself.

Raising one hand, he admired the subtle changes already occurring—the long nails, hard and dark blue as if death itself had already claimed him; the tufts of hair on his hands; the slitted pupils which glowed as yellow as the moon. All these changes disappeared with the breaking of the sun on the horizon but would reappear again once nighttime fell.

Flames engulfed the motorcycle one hundred feet down the road. He stood like a trapeze artist, balancing on the broad limb, dancing in the moonlight as he held his prize aloft.

Dagger stared at the face on the computer screen. He had scanned in Paul Addison's face and Emailed it to Skizzy to have him check gun and voter registrations in the computer. Sergeant Flynn had already checked the Bureau of Motor

Vehicles to see what fictitious name Addison might be using now. But it still listed his old address in Indianapolis and he hadn't renewed his license.

It was a handsome face that stared back at him, sandy-colored hair, fair complexion. He looked much younger than his thirty years and probably was still carded in bars. Stats said Addison was five-foot-ten-inches tall and weighed one-hundred-and-fifty pounds. Didn't sound like a bruiser. How could anyone believe this frail-looking guy could haul a woman's body up a tree? Especially a woman Lisa's size?

Dagger sent Skizzy an Email to tell him he would be stopping by at seven o'clock in the morning and to be up and ready. They had work to do.

Work to do. Dagger rubbed his hands across his face, stood and stretched. Checking the clock, he wondered where Sara was. He turned off the light. The glow from the computer was temporary. Although he leaves his computer on all night, the screen saver would turn the monitor off in fifteen minutes.

Walking past the aviary, Dagger stopped. There were bars in front of the windows to keep Einstein from accidentally flying into them, and there was also a perch in case he wanted to peer out. It was past midnight. Einstein should be asleep on one of the tree branches. Instead, the macaw was perched in front of the window.

Dagger slid the doors open and stepped inside the darkened room. He could tell by the way Einstein's head slowly moved back and forth that the macaw was still awake.

"Hey, Bud. Aren't you supposed to be asleep?" He

stared up at the perch. Einstein kept peering out. Dagger held his arm up and whistled softly. "Einstein."

The macaw turned his gaze to Dagger and after several seconds flew off the perch and clamped his claws onto Dagger's arm. Dagger carried the macaw into the kitchen where the lighting was better.

"Can't sleep?" He handed Einstein a Brazil nut. Einstein eyed it briefly, then turned his head, looked toward the kitchen windows. "Not feeling well?" Dagger checked the macaw's wings for molt and black spots. Next he checked its nostrils, listened to its breathing, checked its eyes for conjunctivitis. Einstein's body shuddered and Dagger heard something splatter on the floor.

Einstein was usually very clean and had been taught to go in a specific area of the aviary. Now the bird had diarrhea, a sure sign that something was wrong. Dagger carried him back to the aviary and set him by the perch just inside the doorway.

Dagger offered him a cheese curl, one of the macaw's favorite treats. Einstein looked away. "That's definitely not a good sign." He stroked Einstein's back. "I'm going to leave you here just for a few minutes while I clean up the mess you made."

Einstein immediately flew back to the perch in front of the window.

Sara? Einstein is sick.
What's wrong with him?
Dagger explained the symptoms
I'm on my way.

* * *

The killer jerked his head up. Why was he hearing voices again? He had heard them last night but dismissed it as part of his enhanced sense of hearing, that maybe the voices were coming from people nearby. And it was the same name—Sara. The sounds were all around him, giving no indication how close or how far the people were. How could that be? Could someone know of his existence? But they weren't speaking to him. It felt more like he was eavesdropping on their conversation.

He scurried through the trees searching for human forms, vehicles, a source for the voices. But there weren't any. What had been said last night? Of course. The weapons. Who was it Sara had been speaking to? He remained silent, hoping to catch more words, more names. But they were silent. What does it mean? Was someone psychic? But that didn't work on him. He had tested it out before, found a supposed psychic and tried speaking to her during one of his spells. How funny he would use that term. His mother used to use that term to describe his grandfather. But the psychic was of no use. Another phony. She paid for her deception. He would have to check around town. But which town? How close was this Sara? How powerful was she? A sudden shot practically jolted him off the limb. What if she were like him?

* * *

Sara ran down the stairs barefoot and dressed in warm ups. She usually showered after being out but wanted to see Einstein.

"Where is he?"

Dagger pointed to the aviary. "He just keeps staring out the windows."

"Would you make him some camomile tea?" Sara clapped her hands softly. "Einstein, I've got something for you."

Einstein flew down to the perch closest to her.

"Come on out here." She stepped over to Dagger's desk. Einstein followed and clamped his claws onto the perch near the desk. "Let me see." She went through the same examination Dagger had—checking the nostrils, feathers, beak. She scratched between the base of the upper beak and ear opening. This caused a yawning reflex. "Say ahhhh." Sara laughed as Einstein yawned.

Dagger came in with a bowl of camomile tea. "How does he look to you?"

Einstein grabbed a beak full of Sara's hair. "No, no," she scolded, pulling her long hair back and twisting it to keep it out of the way. "How were the droppings? Any blood?"

"No, just messy."

"Has he been out lately? Eaten anything strange?" Dagger shook his head no to each question. Sara glanced quickly at him. "Sheila hasn't visited, has she?"

"No." A slight smile tugged at the corners of his mouth. Sheila didn't like Einstein and she liked Sara even less, but he doubted even she would be so calloused as to poison the bird. Dagger stood back, arms crossed. Einstein reached one claw out to him. Dagger's brows furrowed. He held the bowl of tea up to him. "What about that vitamin deficiency disease?" Dagger suggested.

"Avitaminosis? I don't think so. We don't freeze his food and he gets a pretty good variety of foods. Have you ever seen him act this way before?" Sara ran a hand down the bright scarlet feathers, lifted the blue tips of the wings. The feathers were silky to the touch. As a test, she turned him away from the windows. Slowly, Einstein turned back, his head craning to see the panel of windows in the front and then up to the skylights. She felt a shudder run through his body. Slowly, Sara followed Einstein's gaze.

"There was something strange going on when I was out tonight," she said.

Dagger let the macaw climb on his arm and nuzzle under his chin. "How's that?"

"It was silent. I didn't hear or see any wildlife, as if every creature were in hiding."

"Doesn't that usually happen just before a storm?"

"But it isn't raining yet. And the forest should be filled with deer." She watched the tenderness Dagger showed toward Einstein, the gentle way he rubbed the macaw's crown, the genuine concern that caused the tiny crease between Dagger's eyebrows. She caught his gaze and whispered, as if not wanting Einstein to hear. "There's something out there, Dagger. And Einstein knows it."

12

October 10, 7:02 a.m.

He could see between the waffle weave of the box and almost wished he couldn't. The screams were deafening but there wasn't enough room for him to clap his hands over his ears. He tried closing his eyes tight but he wanted to be ready to run if the monster saw him. It was searching, panting from room to room, sniffing, as if it could smell his body scent. Listening, as if it could hear his breathing or his heart beating.

He had seen creatures like this in comic books—the hairy body, misshapen head, feet large and clawed, and when it walked it took unusual leaping paces. Its hands were also unusually large with razor-sharp talons. The eyes, so large. Pupils yellow and slitted, like a cat's, but these were ringed in blood red. Now it swiveled its large head toward the playroom, cocked its head as it sized up the storage chest. Its hideous mouth grinned with realization and it took three long steps toward his hiding place.

"NO!" Sherlock jerked to a sitting position. The door connecting the two hotel rooms flew open and Marty stood in his checkered boxer shorts, dark socks pulled up to his knees, a basketball-shaped stomach curling over the edge, and a Glock 9mm held between his hands, finger on the trigger.

"What the hell?!!" Marty lowered his gun and leaned against the doorjamb. "I am going to have a coronary hanging around you."

"Sorry." Sherlock swung his legs over the side of the bed and took shakey gulps of air. He wore just pajama bottoms, dark and silky. "Damn nightmares. Always the same." He stumbled to the table where his laptop and notes lay.

"Should try getting more than a couple hours sleep," Marty said.

"Not if that's all I see when I close my eyes."

"I already made some coffee." Marty went back into his room and returned several minutes later wearing dark blue pants, unbuttoned shirt hanging loose over his pants, and carrying a mug of coffee. "You take it black, right?"

"Yeah." Sherlock reached up to rake a hand through his hair when he noticed the palm of his hand caked in blood.

"What happened here?" Marty grabbed Sherlock's hand.

Sherlock put his glasses on and studied the injury. The cut was jagged and started to bleed again when he touched it. "I think I cut it on a glass."

* * *

"This better be good. Getting me up at the crack of dawn." Skizzy settled in behind his computer and turned his chair to face Dagger's. He leaned back, arms folded across his unbuttoned camouflage shirt exposing a tattered undershirt. He hardly blinked as Dagger retold the story given to him last night by Sergeant Marty Flynn and Professor Sherlock. When Dagger finished, Skizzy seemed to work his tongue inside his mouth, sucked air through a gap between two front teeth, then muttered, "Done?"

Dagger shrugged as Skizzy turned to his computer to see what last night's database search found. After a few seconds, Dagger said, "You don't seem very surprised."

"Nothing surprises me any more." His gaze shifted so quickly back to Dagger, it seemed as if his eyes were tethered to his head by elastic. "Just like nothing surprises you any more." Shifting just as quickly back to the computer screen, Skizzy mumbled, "It's probably some damn government experiment got loose. Although in all those old werewolf movies, if you are scratched or bitten by one, you become one. I'd keep an eye on that Sherlock guy if I were you."

"Sergeant Flynn already checked him up one side and down the other."

"And we know how thorough cops can be."

Dagger shook the cobwebs from his head and poured two cups of coffee from the thermos he brought, shoved one toward Skizzy. A pamphlet pinned to the bulletin board on the wall caught his attention. He lifted the top page and studied it.

Dagger said, "Isn't this the census form that was supposed to be returned months ago?"

Without looking away from the monitor, Skizzy replied, "Yep. And that's where it's staying. What the hell does Big Brother need to know what kinda plumbing I got, how much I pay for gas, what time I leave for work? For what? So someone can rob the place while I'm gone?"

Dagger smiled at his friend, his gaze sweeping the makeshift bunker in the workroom beneath Skizzy's Pawn Shop.

In between the pounding of the keyboard, Skizzy asked, "Did you fill one out?"

"Uhhh." Dagger smiled behind the rim of his cup. "Simon must have lost it in the mail."

"Where's Sara today? Thought she might be coming with you."

Everyone expected Sara to be with him, at least the men. They couldn't get enough of her. Her youthful innocence was refreshing. Sheila preferred he not be seen with Sara, any time, anywhere. Sheila had a green streak the size of Texas, but he refused to listen to her urgings which bordered on demanding, that he find some place else to live and work.

Dagger said, "I asked Sara to take Einstein to the parrot doctor. He's been acting strange lately."

"Pity." Skizzy touched several more keys and pointed to the screen. "This Paul Addison disappeared off the face of the earth in 1998. There are several thousand dudes somewhat identical in description but nothing exact. No charge cards. No employment I.D.s with a match."

"Try disguises. Brown hair, mustache, maybe long hair."

"Needle in a haystack," Skizzy muttered. He brought Paul Addison's picture back up on the screen. There was something eerie about his stare. The pupils were black holes, pinpoints with nothing behind them. "Guy's got what my Pappy called doll's eyes. Ain't no life behind them. Soulless."

Dagger clasped his hands behind his head and leaned back. Skizzy was right. The youthful, innocent face Dagger had seen on his screen last night did have that eerie quality. "Like Ed Gein and Charlie Manson," he said.

Skizzy tapped a few keys and placed a box around that portion of the face. "I could try to match up the eyes only. Although there are probably thousands in our prisons now with them eyes." He mumbled under his breath, a conversation with himself. "Probably clonings done by the government, maybe the only thing they couldn't change was them eyes. All the clones got the same eyes." He lifted a paper plate under his chin as he took a bite of the homemade cranberry nut bread Dagger had brought. Fresh from Sara's kitchen. He brushed crumbs from his chin, careful that none fell on his keyboard. "Could search for every new home buyer and renter since ninety-eight in Northwest Indiana and the entire Chicagoland area. Though I think I'll need to buy another box of printer paper."

"There has to be an easier way to narrow our search." Dagger shielded his eyes from the bright fluorescent bulbs hugging the ceiling. Elbow on the table he slumped down in the chair and pressed a fist to his chin. He fingered the remains of several Micks lying in an empty cigar box. He heard Skizzy's chair roll over to another computer and more clicking of keys. Several seconds later he heard a whooshing noise but was too exhausted to lift his head. He didn't even flinch when a dragonfly coasted over, turned and swayed, like a hang glider running out of steam.

"Damn, you really must be tired." Skizzy punched a few more keys and the dragonfly landed on the table.

"Just like the details of this case didn't surprise you, well, nothing I see in this place surprises me." The object was life size and when its delicate wings settled down, Dagger picked up the dragonfly and examined the metal insect. "Audio, visual?"

Skizzy explained, "Not yet. It's aerodynamically correct. Scientists have found a way to duplicate the movements of flying insects. I hacked into the government boys' site. Built me one but don't know yet how they plan to use them."

Dagger's eyes slowly surveyed the room. "Where you hiding the controls?"

Skizzy tapped the keyboard and the dragonfly took off. "Just like the Micks."

Dagger said, "Too bad you can't train it to be a hunting dog. Give it a sniff of a suspect and let him find the guy."

Skizzy tapped the computer mouse, maneuvering the dragonfly to a bookcase, but he misjudged the height of the shelving. The metal insect clanged against the edge and clattered to the floor. "That's why. Needs to be perfected." He rolled his chair back to the first computer, the wheels clattering along the linoleum. He tapped the mouse and the screen came to life. "I checked our Micks."

Dagger turned his attention to the surveillance tapes from the Evidence Room. "No one suspicious?" he asked.

"Nope." Skizzy shoved another piece of bread in his mouth and wiped the crumbs with the back of his hand. "No one walked away with any weapons." He washed it down with a slug of coffee then grabbed a vacuum the size of a toothbrush and ran it over the keyboard. "Just regular shit and everyone accessed it using the scanner. No one jimmied a lock or nothin'."

Another monitor embedded in the wall buzzed. The screen showed two youths hanging around the outside of the store. The sleeves of their tee shirts had been cut off revealing colorful art tattoos on their upper arms. One had a loop earring in his eyebrow. They both looked like they ran out of money before the barber could finish the job. Their heads were shaved accept for a patch of hair on the top which was long and pulled back in a ponytail.

The front door to Skizzy's Pawn Shop was kept locked. And any time anyone was near the entrance, a monitor would sound.

"This should be fun." Skizzy pressed a button. His voice blared through the intercom outside the door. "What do you two want?" The two boys jumped back, looked around the door to see where the voice was coming from. "I don't sell drugs and I don't sell weapons. State your business," Skizzy barked. The two youths took off. "Damn kids," he muttered. "Look at how the hell they got their hair. Like they didn't know whether they wanted a buzz cut or a Mohawk."

Dagger laughed, eyeing his friend whose random tufts of

gray hair looked as if he had experimented with a pair of scissors himself or had gotten too close to the barbecue grill. "You're having way too much fun with that." He pressed the heels of his palms to his eyes. He should probably be glad it wasn't warm in the room because he could very easily take a nap.

"Why are you so tired?" Skizzy passed the thermos of coffee to Dagger. A little gleam glistened in his eyes. "Sara keeping you up?"

Dagger just stared blankly at yet another friend with innuendo and winky-winky type comments. Finally, he said, "I told you, Einstein wasn't feeling good."

"Uh huh, uh huh." Skizzy turned his attention back to the computer. "Well, lookie here," he said, pointing to the screen. "We only have ourselves about thirty-six-hundred matches in the sick eyes category. Want my advice?"

Dagger blinked slowly, almost afraid to ask, suspecting exactly what he was going to say.

Skizzy leaned in, whispered as if his own walls had listening devices. "You gotta bring him to you."

13

October 10, 8:12 a.m.

Marty Flynn clutched his take-out cup as if attempting to draw some heat through the fibers. He stared at Professor Sherlock in his herringbone sportscoat, V-neck sweater and starched shirt collar. He almost expected him to pull out a pipe to complete the picture. Sherlock paced in back of the wooden horses which had been erected to keep traffic from flowing through Camden Parkway. Drivers were being re-routed to Route 12.

Just a routine traffic accident, according to the police scanner. But Sherlock had convinced Marty that there could be a little more to even the most routine accident.

Nature had left its icy breath on shaded patches of grass, and the pavement was littered with wind-swept leaves.

"Sorry I'm late," Padre said when he approached. "Come on. Walk with me." He rushed past them forcing the two men to run to keep up. "Had a meeting this morning with the damn politicians. They want something done fast on the Lisa Cambridge homicide." He flicked away his cigarette butt. "They don't care who we arrest just so long as the residents feel the streets are safe. Damn elections."

"You don't have any suspects though, right?" Marty aimed his empty coffee cup toward a fifty-gallon drum and it bounced on the lip and dropped into the can.

They could see the cluster of techs two hundred yards down the road. "Best we can tell," Padre started, "is the motorcycle was hit by another vehicle, driver probably drunk, swerved over the center lane. Maybe both drivers were drunk. The driver of the other vehicle didn't even brake. No skid marks, no witnesses. Have to warn you. This ain't a pretty site."

They stopped short of the accident area. This stretch of the woods had pockets which had been carved out to create rest areas with picnic tables close to the road and a pavilion back toward the woods near a portable washroom. The motorcycle was just beyond this open area lying at the base of a large oak tree in a smoldering twist of metal and melted plastic. The driver had been thrown on impact landing fifty feet beyond the wreckage.

A woman with a tight wad of gray curls moved toward the men. Gretchen, the assistant medical examiner for Cedar Point, was a petite, portly figure stuffed into a dark green one-piece coverall, like a toxic waste disposal suit. A pear with legs.

"This your case, Padre?" Gretchen asked.

"Not unless you tell me it's a homicide." Padre introduced Marty and Sherlock to the M.E. She smiled at the mention of Sherlock's name. "They are on a fact-finding mission from Indianapolis." Padre didn't elaborate.

"Should be easy finding this hit-and-run driver." Gretchen stuck an arm in the direction of the crumpled body. "Just look for a car or more likely a semi with this guy's head as a hood ornament."

"Wonderful." Padre looked at the two men. "Satisfied?"

Sherlock chewed on the inside of his bottom lip, dragged his gaze from the splayed body to the road behind. He slowly started moving back down the road.

"Hey," Marty called out. With a shrug toward Padre, he said, "Just give us a few minutes."

Marty caught up with Sherlock as Padre trailed behind. Sherlock stayed on the right side of the road, his eyes tracking the trail of blood on the left. "Makes sense," Marty said. "Semi hits the guy back there, carries his head on his grill for a hundred feet."

Padre turned and looked back down the road toward the wreckage. "Could have hit him from behind, though. Pushed the bike into the pole and carried the head the rest of the way."

"But there isn't a second set of tire tracks," Sherlock pointed out. "None anywhere. And that ground is soft. There should be something." Sherlock squinted at the bright light filtering between the leaves and continued walking, stopping suddenly.

"This is where the blood stopped," Padre pointed out. The trail of blood ended at the pavement directly across from them.

The men looked further down the road on the soft shoulder. No skid marks, tire tracks or ruts to indicate anyone went off the road.

"There is another scenario," Padre said rubbing the back of his neck. "The motorcycle went out of control, driver lost his head...pardon the pun...and it was left in the street for the next vehicle to come by. Probably stuck to the undercarriage." A shudder sliced through his body. He studied the professor's furrowed brows. "Why would you try to make something out of a gruesome, freak traffic accident?"

"Because it comes so close to Friday. I'm suspicious of all deaths. Call me cautious."

"That you are." Padre twisted his head left to right and rubbed the back of his neck. "Damn mattress. Gotta have the wife buy a new one." He dropped his head, twisted left and right, then tilted it back. He opened his eyes as a whisper of a breeze parted the branches overhead. A spotlight of sun danced between the leaves. Padre's mouth gaped. "Sweet mother of god!" He made a sign of the cross.

The roar of the Harley echoed through the woods. Dagger maneuvered the black-as-sin Sport between two squad cars and brought it to rest on the shoulder. The motorcycle had been another payment for services rendered when a client didn't have money to pay Dagger. Two things Dagger had liked about it. It had batwing fairing and black ceramic-coated pipes. He no sooner turned the key, swung one long leg over the bike, and popped the side stand, then a familiar blur of platinum broke out of the crowd.

Sheila pushed the sleeves up on her red leather jacket as she rushed over. Dagger wondered how on earth she could bend over in a skirt that short. She did have great legs, he had to say that much for her. And she knew it. Modesty was not one of Sheila's strong points.

Dagger walked toward the barricade, his eyes taking in the crowd from behind his dark sunglasses. Force of habit. All Padre told him was to get over here quick. No details but Dagger had a sick feeling in his stomach. Now he had to contend with Sheila.

Dagger folded back the sleeves of his black quilted shirt and pressed forward, forcing Sheila to rush to keep up with him. He pulled his glasses down and peered at her exposed legs. "You're going to catch cold."

Sheila smiled seductively as she pulled on his shirt-sleeve. "Maybe you can keep me warm. What's up? What are you doing here?"

"I needed to ask Padre something and he told me to stop by because his batteries were running low on his cellular." Dagger glanced at the number of cars, the cop directing traffic fifty feet away, photographers with camcorders perched on their shoulders, the M.E. wagon, Crime Tech van, a man and his two sons, and several other curiosity seekers the cops had yet to push back. Padre was waiting at the barricades for him.

"Well, Miss Monroe. Daddy sends you out now to cover hit-and-runs?" Padre's eyes smiled but his face was as gray as the concrete road.

"What's going on, Sergeant?" Sheila asked.

Ignoring Sheila, Padre motioned for Dagger to follow him.

"Freedom of the press, dammit!" Sheila yelled at their

backs.

"What's up?" Dagger asked when they were a safe distance from Sheila.

"Another victim. You won't believe this."

As they walked the stretch of road, Dagger noticed techs clustered around a fire truck. Padre continued one hundred feet past the fire truck to a smoking tangle of metal. Rooted nearby was Sergeant Flynn, whose trench coat had added a few more wrinkles.

Dagger observed the body being loaded onto the gurney and studied the rubble lying on its side, a front fender of the motorcycle lay near the body undamaged. "What a waste."

Padre jammed his fists into his pockets. "Every death is a waste."

"I'm talking about the Fat Boy. That Harley's so new I can smell the paint from here."

Marty scoffed at the comment and yelled, "Well, it ain't new no more."

They walked back to where Marty stood as Dagger asked Padre, "Where's the professor?"

"Things were starting to get to him. Said he had to take a breather." Padre started walking toward the fire truck as a snorkel was slowly being raised.

Dagger found it curious that the fire truck was a distance from the motorcycle. Even though the fire had been extinguished, he would think they would want to stay close in case something flared up.

"What's with the fire truck?"

Padre tugged at Dagger's shirt and pointed skyward. With a chuckle, Dagger complied, slowly lifting his head almost expecting some squirrel sacrificed and hanging from a limb. But then he saw the head of a man impaled on a thin wayward stump jutting vertically from a larger limb. He removed his sunglasses and slowly walked in a circle, getting a view from all angles. It was a large head, he guessed the owner had to have been at least two hundred and fifty pounds. His forehead reached back beyond his hairline, long thinning hair matted with a dark, red substance. The eyes were wide, pupils staring skyward, mouth gaping. It wasn't a pretty sight.

He tugged on his earring as he dropped his gaze to the two men. "Guy's got his head in the clouds."

Marty scoffed again. "Don't you take anything seriously?"

Dagger chewed on one arm of his sunglasses and glared at the cop. "Yes I do. I take seriously the fact that your boy seems to know an awful lot about these cases. And exactly where was he last night?"

"Now wait a minute." Marty's blaring voice caused heads to turn.

"Did he have any scratches on him? Blood?"

Marty opened his mouth to retaliate, but snapped his jaws shut and stared at his feet.

Curious, Dagger jerked his gaze to Padre. "He did, didn't he."

"He said he cut his hand on a glass," Padre explained. He placed a hand on each of their shoulders, a ring announcer giving last minute instructions. "Just keep your voices down. Marty checked the professor out thoroughly."

Dagger shoved his glasses onto the bridge of his nose and jammed his fist onto his waist, his gaze drifting back to the trees. There was one sick bastard running around and it wouldn't be the first time a killer had the support of a cop. "What does the M.E. say?"

Motioning toward the portly green pear, Padre said, "Gretchen examined the, uh, rest of the body. She decided to call Luther in on this one. Not that she doesn't trust herself. She just feels it needs two opinions."

Dagger looked at the disheveled cop. Marty was scuffling his feet, rubbing the back of his neck, avoiding Dagger's eyes.

"Who found it?" Dagger asked, nodding his head toward the branches overhead.

Padre and Marty exchanged glances. Finally Padre admitted, "The professor actually. Gretchen at first thought the deceased was the victim of a hit and run and the other vehicle was riding around with the guy's head as a hood ornament. But the professor doubted it and started walking the street, trying to re-enact the scene. Then he stopped right here, I looked up," Padre lifted his face, "and voila."

Dagger tossed another accusing glare at Marty.

"Believe me, I know what you're thinking," Marty piped up. "Two years ago I had the same doubts. But I would stake my career on Professor Sherlock. He knows what he's talking about. These cases are tearing him up. He doesn't sleep much," Marty added. "Keeps having nightmares. And, for the record, I did find a broken glass in the bathroom wastebasket."

Dagger watched as a lanky black man, close-cropped hair, rushed down the street from the parking lot. Luther had arrived. Known as "Doogie" behind his back because of his youthful appearance, Luther was pushing retirement age.

"Luther's going to be a while with this one." Padre motioned for the two men to follow him back to where their cars were parked.

The three men strolled toward the wooden horses. Dagger still had his doubts about Sherlock but he had to consider other options. "Okay, how about satanic sacrifices, witchcraft. Any new cults in town, Padre?"

"That was one of the first thoughts that popped into my mind." Padre lit a cigarette and flicked the match on the damp asphalt. "I'd almost prefer some flesh and bone guy clothed in a satanic cape to what Sherlock is suggesting. Can't for the life of me get into this shape-shifter theory."

"Press would have a field day with either one," Marty commented, noticing the surge of reporters behind the wooden horses as they approached.

"You need a scapegoat, someone to throw off the press." Dagger slowed his pace, wanting to finish their discussion before they were within earshot of the press. "I think you should arrest J.D. for Lisa's murder."

Padre stopped in mid-stride. "What?"

"Let J.D. know what's up. It's a way to calm the press and more important, let the killer think we aren't on to him."

Marty jerked a thumb over his shoulder. "What about this latest homicide?"

"Hit and run," Dagger said with a shrug. "Gruesome as it may be. You just have to make sure you threaten every cop and tech with suspension if they talk to anyone about what they saw here today."

"What's going on? Who are these men?" Sheila smothered them with questions once they reached the wooden horses.

"Hit and run. I told you before," Padre replied.

"Then why all these cops? And what leads have you had on the Lisa Cambridge case?"

"BACK OFF!" Dagger yelled. "Since when are you covering traffic accidents? Daddy demote you?"

"Fuck you!" Sheila yelled back, slapping her notepad across his arm. She turned on one spiked heel and stormed off.

"She's one we'll have to watch," Padre said.

"Anyone taking a picture of the onlookers?" Dagger whispered as his eyes searched the crowd.

"Yes, one of the supposed reporters with a camera is a cop," Padre whispered back. They were now within full earshot of the press and onlookers, so Padre changed the subject. "How's Einstein feeling?"

Dagger said, "Sara's at the vet with him now."

A face in the crowd, shadowed by mirrored sunglasses, turned toward Dagger at the mention of Sara's name. A thin smile formed across his face.

14

October 10, 10:16 a.m.

"See, that wasn't so bad, was it?" Sara caressed Einstein, holding him close to her as he clung tightly to her arm. "The doctor just took a little blood. There was no need for you to nip at her like that." Einstein stared at her with one yellow-ringed eye. "And to screech out 'bad doctor, bad doctor,' was not very nice of you." She smiled at the macaw. Five years old and he acted like a mischievous child. But since macaws could live to be one hundred, Einstein was basically still a bratty kid.

The Pinehurst Animal Clinic was tucked in an alcove of trees surrounded by vacant land destined for development. Moe's Yard used to sit here, a junk yard where you could find anything from parts for a '55 Mustang to an old time juke box. Moe died two years ago. No relatives. No will. It didn't take long for the state, county, and city to claim the property. The city won.

Pinehurst had one aviary doctor on staff. Although the

main parking lot and entrance were in the front, the entrance to Doctor Mia Wong's office was in the back. The birds were less agitated if they didn't have to deal with cats, dogs, ferrets, raccoons, and sometimes even pigs.

Doctor Wong was fascinated with Einstein, especially his ability to remember things that had happened on past visits. She always said she has never seen a more intelligent macaw. Of course, this always made Dagger beam.

She agreed with Sara that something was frightening Einstein. Dr. Wong took a stool and blood sample, though, to rule out anything more serious. In the meantime, she gave Sara some medicine to put into Einstein's water, more like a sedative. Sara was hesitant to give Einstein drugs but if it would do him more good than harm, especially with what was happening, she was all for it.

Sara had parked the truck in the farthest section of the lot so the truck could be shaded by trees. She immediately noticed two seedy characters leaning against a red pick-up truck also parked in the shade. It had a red cap pocked with rust and several dents in the fenders. They didn't have any animals with them and she doubted any legitimate pet owner would leave his pet alone in the clinic.

Not even noon yet and each guy had a can of beer in his hand. Their dark uniforms were stained with grease or sweat, and the names sewn above the pockets. They were repairmen or maybe mechanics. Two-day growth of stubble on their faces, early twenties, probably still out since last night.

She fumbled with her keys while she made a quick assessment of her own clothing…stretch pants and a thigh-length sweater over a long-sleeved blouse, collar turned up. Not much skin showing yet these guys had lust in their eyes and the scent of it in their sweat. The quarts of beer they had consumed since God knows what time had raised their already high levels of testosterone.

"What a gorgeous bird," one of her admirers said.

Einstein lifted one foot and made a hacking noise.

The two men laughed. "A damn attack parrot to boot. Don't that beat all?" The larger of the two men flung his empty beer can over his shoulder where it bounced off the roof of the truck and clammered to the ground. They were each over two hundred pounds, wrestler size.

Sara unlocked the door and rolled the window down part way. "Stay here and be quiet, Einstein," she whispered, setting her purse on the floor. Once she closed the door, Einstein clamped onto the door handle and climbed up so he could see out.

The two men swaggered over, separating so she had no escape route. "Lookie lookie here, Ted."

They were close enough that Sara could read the names on their pockets. Ted's friend, the talker, was Carl, who looked like he had been in one too many bar fights. His face sported a jagged scar just below his left eye. Bruisers came to mind when she looked at each of them with their wide heads that seemed to sprout right from their shoulders, no necks. They could probably have decent toned bodies if they didn't pollute them with the liquor. She imagined they lived at fast food restaurants, too.

"Have a problem?" Sara asked.

"Oh, yeah." Carl the brawler rubbed his crotch. "I got

one big problem I think you can help me with."

A loud rumble echoed from the side drive as Dagger and his Harley came into view. It didn't take long for him to figure out what was happening. He killed the engine and climbed off.

"What's going on, boys?" He smiled a knowing smile, more of a smirk, at the two lugs.

Ted snapped open a switchblade. "Back off. This is our party."

Setting the side stand, Dagger looked over his shoulder at the back entrance. Too early for lunch so he doubted anyone would be emerging from the back door any time soon. Dagger held his hands up in mock surrender. "No problem. I just want to watch." He grinned, a wide, amused grin, as he lowered his sunglasses and looked at Sara. "Going to need any help, Sweetie?"

Sara assessed the men slowly from head to toe. "I don't think so," she finally said.

The two wrestlers looked at each other and laughed, examined her five-foot-six-inch frame, and chuckled again.

"You better think twice, guys," Dagger said, plopping his sunglasses back on his nose, pulling a can of Pepsi from the cooler on the back of his bike, and settling back on his Harley. He took a swig of pop and marveled how Sara could be an absolute basket case in a crowded mall but put her one-on-one where she had to defend herself and she was a she-cat. He propped his feet on the handlebars, leaned against the back rest, arms crossed, and mumbled mainly to himself, "Let the fun begin."

"Me first." Ted made a step toward Sara and was met

with a quick kick to the groin. He let out a groan and dropped to one knee.

Carl waved his knife at her and motioned toward their vehicle. "Get in the truck."

"I don't think so," Sara replied, circling around the gasping Ted who was struggling to stand. Carl hadn't counted on Sara being so swift. She made a three-hundred-and-sixty-degree turn and was all legs as she kicked the knife from his hand with one foot and planted a kick under his chin with the other, sending him sprawling against a tree.

Carl recovered and grabbed a handful of Sara's hair and yanked. He wrapped a beefy arm around her waist and tried dragging her to his vehicle when she slipped from his grasp like some fish, a trick she had learned practicing Tai Chi with Dagger. She was all arms and legs again, pummeling his out-of-condition body. She finished him off by planting a kick to his fresh scar and flinging him twenty yards where his body literally flew over the cap of the red truck.

By now Ted was scrambling to get back to his truck.

Dagger applauded, slow and deliberate. "I warned you boys to think twice."

A figure parked in a Chevy Nova along the east side of the building watched in shock and amazement at the scene taking place in the back lot. He was concealed behind a dumpster.

"Such power," he whispered. "How does she do it? Throw a body that size twenty yards? Who and what are you, Sara?" He pulled down his mirrored sunglasses and eyed Dagger. He hadn't quite figured out who Dagger was yet. A cop? Undercover? Homicide? Why was he at the crime scene? Arriving on his big Harley, his tall, muscular body. He hated guys who acted as if they were God's gift to society, not to mention women. Probably ex-military, fuckin' Navy Seal, CIA, I- know-everything motherfucker. Even that one reporter, what was her name? Sheila, yeah, was clinging to him like some pathetic whiner. He hated women who whined. There had been so many whiners he had silenced. Just a couple nights ago he had picked up one in a Chicago bar.

The moon had loomed over the trees as he loomed over her. She was in the throes of passion when the energy surged through him, changed his eyes. Her pleadings were so pathetic. But she couldn't scream, not with his hands wrapped tightly around her neck, crushing her larynx.

There was very little in the Chicago papers the next day. Just another dead slut. So many of them in the bars, hanging on guys, flirting, wearing revealing clothing, then trying to act like they aren't *that kind of girl* when they take you home.

And guys, the ones like Dagger, who think society can't survive without their skills or their brains, and women can't survive without him. He's killed many like him, crushed them, had them begging for mercy. Dagger. DAMN. That was the person Sara was communicating with the first night he had heard the voices. It didn't look like Dagger left Sara's side too often. Were they married? Lovers? Is that why the blond reporter was clinging to him? Jealousy maybe, of the young, exotic beauty?

He watched as Dagger lowered the hydraulic lift on the back of the truck and loaded his big-ass Harley onto it. Dagger strapped the cycle in and then hoisted himself easily over the side. "Goddam showoff," the man muttered. His fingers gripped the upholstered seat as he watched Dagger cup Sara's face in his hands, smile at her, probably telling her how well she handled those jerks. She smiled at him, a loving, trusting smile. What the hell were they to each other? He obviously knew her skills. Did they know he existed? He didn't like being in the dark, not knowing the answers. He had to separate them. He had to get rid of Dagger.

By noon Chief John Wozniak held a press conference at which time it was announced that John "J.D." Draper had been arrested for the murder of Officer Lisa Cambridge. He was being held without bond in the county jail. Chief Wozniak answered only a few questions stating simply it had been a crime of passion. No details of how the body was found were released, nor were details about this morning's supposed hit-and-run.

J.D. understood his role in the game and would receive full pay during his time away from work. He was housed in an isolated room on the top floor at Headquarters instead of a cell. It was an executive suite reserved for visiting dignitaries and even had its own gym and kitchen. He was given a computer and case files Lisa had worked on to see if he could compile a list of people with a grudge and determine if any had been released from prison recently. Doc Abrams promised to bring Max by for a visit. She thought it would do the dog good to see a familiar face.

Sitting behind his desk, Chief Wozniak stared at the reports in front of him, then at Professor Sherlock, Sergeant Marty Flynn, and finally, Sergeant Martinez.

Several strands of red hair drifted onto Wozniak's forehead and he brushed it back with a freckled hand. "I don't believe I am sitting here half-believing what is in these reports." He stared at Padre. "Can you honestly tell me you have exhausted all conceivable avenues? Escaped convicts? Local serial killers? Cultists?" Turning his gaze to Marty and Sherlock, the chief said, "You come into my town with some fairy tale story and expect me to swallow it?" His gaze swung back to Padre. "And you believe this shit?"

Padre looked over at his two companions, the shade of gray that hadn't left Sherlock's face since they found the motorcyclist's head, the near-retirement Marty Flynn who could have taken early retirement at any time but was supporting Sherlock like a follower of a religious fanatic.

"I spent ten years in a parochial school being taught to believe in something I couldn't see." Padre let those words settle in. "Did I ever tell you the real reason I left the seminary, John?" He leaned back in the posh chair, glanced above the chief's shoulder where a picture of the two of them from a fishing trip hung. Padre studied his hands in thought. He had always told people it was a last minute change of heart after taking a course in law enforcement.

"It really isn't that hard to get people to believe in God," Padre continued. "The parents enroll kids in catechism where they learn that God is good, God rewards them for being good, God punishes those who are evil. But then you grow up and you realize God doesn't punish the evil. That it's up to society to punish the evil. People see the likes of Gacy, Dahmer, Speck, Gein, it's a damn laundry list. We all sit back and wait for lightning to strike them. But it doesn't. It strikes the innocent child with leukemia, a young mother with breast cancer, the father of six with a head-on collision."

"So you lost your faith in God?" John asked.

Padre shook his head no. "I just don't think he has all the control everyone gives him credit for. You can't have the image of a man in your head when you think of God because man has too many imperfections." Padre twirled his wedding band as he spoke. "There is a power out there, call it force of nature if you want. God can only do so much. It's up to us to remove the evil from society. Just as I can't say what possessed Gein to dance in the moonlight wearing the skin of his victims, I can't say what is possessing this…" he looked over at Sherlock whose hands were clasped and eyes closed as if in prayer, "killer to do what he does. All I can do is try to stop…it."

Sherlock's eyes opened, as though prayer time were over. There was silence in the room as Chief Wozniak pondered Padre's words. After several minutes he asked them, "What is your game plan?"

The three men sitting in front of Wozniak's desk searched each other's faces, moved around uncomfortably. Marty Flynn cleared his throat and mumbled, "We don't have one."

15

October 10, 1:05 p.m.

"Just leave it be," Leyton Monroe barked.

"But, that's how many homicides this year? Fifteen? And it's only October. We never have more than seven or eight."

Leyton pulled the cigar from his hog-jowled face and pointed a finger at his daughter. "The breaking news is the corruption at City Hall." He set his cigar in an ashtray and shuffled the papers on his cluttered desk. He found what he was looking for and handed it to her. "I have it on good authority that the feds are going to arrest Building Inspector Andrew Lesner for bribery and extortion. You be on top of it."

Sheila studied her father's notes with little interest. She placed the report in her lap. "Dadddddyy." She strung out his name like an eight-year-old trying to get a new bike out of her father. "First, the cops are very hush hush about the woman officer."

"They already arrested her boyfriend. Shoulda known better than to mix races," he added under his breath. He jammed his cigar in his mouth and leaned back in his Corinthian leather chair.

"And the hit and run," Sheila plodded on. "There's more to that. Sergeant Martinez brings in an Indianapolis cop and some professor from Purdue University. Not to mention, Martinez has been meeting secretly with Dagger and then calls him out to the crime scene."

Leyton sprung forward at the mention of Dagger's name. "So that's what this is about? You stay as far away from that no class detective as you can. Hasn't he caused you enough grief? Leaving you stranded at the altar." He gazed down at the ring on his daughter's left hand. "You are making an absolute fool of yourself over him. GIVE IT UP." He pointed toward the door. "Now go work on a real case or I'll just give the damn story to Caroline."

Sheila stormed out of her father's office and slammed the door. She walked past Caroline's desk and barked, "In my office." One thing Sheila had always been good at was giving an assignment to an assistant and then putting her name on the by-line. Her father always stood by her, believed it was his daughter who actually wrote the story. Now was a good time to indoctrinate her new assistant in Sheila's version of the *Monroe Doctrine*.

* * *

The tattooed remains of Simeon 'Tex' Miller lay on tables four and five in the medical examiner's office. It was a full house with Senior Examiner Luther Jamison, Gretchen, Chief Wozniak, Padre, Flynn, and Sherlock.

It was too macabre seeing a head on one table and the body on another. Tex had been a big man, his torso looking like a huge mound of dirt covered by a sheet. Luther pulled the sheet down to the victim's waist. A scene of the crucifixion was tattooed on his chest, angels floated near clouds, two women wept at the feet of Christ. On each of his arms was a tattoo of a serpent being impaled with an arrow.

Luther pointed to the neck of the deceased. It wasn't a clean cut. Part of the spine and muscles were exposed. "Really bizarre markings." The M.E. pointed to four wounds on each side of the neck.

The men leaned closer, studied the bruised puncture wounds.

"What do you think made them?" Chief Wozniak asked

Luther peered at the men over his square bifocals and shrugged his bony shoulders. "Could take a stab at it but you'd think I was insane."

"Try us," Marty said, averting his curious gaze to the head on the next table.

"Okay." Luther studied the body, hesitated, glanced at each of the men, shrugged his bony shoulders again, like a wrestler trying to determine the best way to approach his opponent. Then he held his hands out, palms up, fingers extended and pointed directly at the location of the wounds.

"If you were Mulder and Scully, I'd have no problem telling you with a straight face that this guy's head was literally lifted right off his body."

"Talons," Sherlock whispered.

"Jezzus." The word floated from Chief Wozniak's mouth on a lengthy exhale.

It was so still in the room that the ticking of the clock above the door echoed like a bass drum. They stared at the remains as if each were trying to come up with a more logical explanation. Padre studied the image of the crucifixion. "Looks like lightning struck the wrong person again."

Einstein was chatty as ever and seemed in good spirits. So Sara didn't put the medicine in his water. She set out bowls of fresh vegetables and fruit for Einstein and then closed the aviary door.

Dagger was in the kitchen on the phone with Padre and when he hung up he kept staring at the phone.

"Bad news?"

Dagger turned and forced a smile. "Did I tell you how great you handled those two idiots?"

She eyed him suspiciously. "Yes, you did, and what did Padre say?" She trailed after him as he walked to his desk and sat down behind the keyboard. Crossing her arms, she waited while Dagger sifted through yellow sticky notes dotting the desk. "Well?" she tried again.

Dagger leaned back in his chair and studied the young woman. Thoughts of how she handled the two men in the parking lot brought a smile to his face. He wished he could be a fly on the wall when those two yokels retold the story to friends.

"It's a little bizarre."

"What else is new?" She gathered her thick hair to one side and braided it while Dagger told her Luther's explanation of what had happened to Tex Miller. When he got to the part about his head being lifted off of his body, her fingers paused in mid-braid. "Lifted off?"

"Yep. Padre saw the puncture marks. Of course, Sherlock believes they were caused by foot-long talons." Dagger laughed, still not quite sure what to make of the case. He dialed Skizzy's number and waited for his face to pop up on the monitor.

"Skizzy, how is the investigation going? Have you narrowed it down any?"

"Well, gee, give me more than ten minutes why don't you?"

"Don't have ten minutes to spare. We've got people dropping like flies."

"I've got Micks running all over the place, reports cluttering up my floor, a dang sicko werewolf running around." There was a slight pause. "This a secure line?"

"Always. What did you find? Did you narrow it down any?"

"Just hold your pants on." On the screen, Skizzy was shifting through papers until he found what he wanted. "I used your photo of the Paul Addison dude to compare to drivers license photos, gun registration photos, and any other I.D.s. Got weight, height, all other pertinent poop. Eliminated suspects currently incarcerated, and my list in the age range given is about six-hundred-and-eighty-seven."

"Eliminate those buying a house. I think this guy is a transient who will strictly rent."

"What about birth date?" Sara asked. "When did Professor Sherlock say Paul Addison was born?"

Dagger peered under stacks of folders looking for notes. Sara handed him a file folder with Paul Addison's name on it. She had already made a case file. She was too damn organized. "Thanks," he mouthed. To Skizzy he said, "Focus on those who have given a birth date of November 13, 1970."

"Nice time to tell me that. And all fine and good if they all filled out personal information. What else?"

"Any activity with our Micks?"

"Not yet but I'll be monitoring it all afternoon and evening."

"I'll keep mine on, too." They said their good-byes and Skizzy's face faded from the screen.

Sara looked at the calendar on Dagger's desk and then the clock. "I'm going to go lie down for a while."

He watched her climb the stairs. Ten minutes later he was serving coffee to Simon in the kitchen.

"Is this a quiz?" Simon said over the rim of his cup.

"Sort of." Dagger dragged a stool around to the other side of the counter across from his friend. "I've gone over it myself. I'm just trying to get a different perspective."

"Shoot."

"If you didn't want anyone to find you, other than changing your name, hair color, and all your identifications, what would you do?"

Simon stared at him for the longest time, his gaze shifting to his surroundings as though studying the furnishings for the first time, then the outside property. His gaze rested back on Dagger's face.

His voice was soft, the twinkle in his eyes gone. In almost a whisper, Simon said, "That's a strange question coming from you, Dagger."

Dagger stared at his friend who seemed to always know what was going on in town but in the five years he had known him, had never pried into Dagger's past, never pestered him with the *what* and *why fors*. Dagger had rented office space above a bar, no lease, no paperwork. Never advertised his business. It was all word of mouth.

Dagger's dark eyes were just as serious and in a deadpan voice, the edges of his lips curling up in a smile, said, "Humor me."

"Wouldn't pack a lot of clothes. Travel light."

"What else."

"Get a fictitious occupation, something low profile, like a delivery guy, writer maybe, a job I can do at home." Simon took another sip of coffee in thought, then continued. "I'd probably move in with someone whose name is already on the lease." He paused a few beats, then added, "What's up?"

Dagger filled him in on the *full moon* case. He watched his friend's movements, hands frozen to his cup, eyes bulged over the rim.

"Full moon and a Friday the thirteenth?" Simon set his cup down, his burly head shaking. "Can't you ever get a dull case?"

16

October 10, 5:05 p.m.

Skizzy shoveled a forkful of prime rib into his mouth, a culinary gift from Dagger who had found a supplier, a farmer who didn't believe in injecting his cattle with growth hormones. Dagger would purchase half a cow to stock both his and Skizzy's freezers. The meat was tender and the baked potato had been cooking in the oven for the past hour.

He was attaching pages of his suspect search to an Email to Dagger while the other monitor kept a close eye on the Micks in the Evidence Room. He clicked on SEND for the Email to Dagger and ran upstairs for salt. By the time he returned, the Email attachment had uploaded and Skizzy signed off of the Internet. A movement on the other monitor made him jerk his head around. Someone was in the Evidence Room.

"Well, well. We have a visitor."

The man was youthful looking and was wearing a brown uniform and baseball cap. Skizzy dialed Dagger's phone to see if he was watching. All he got was a recording. He hung up and decided to wait and watch to see if anything happened that was worth reporting. Then he would call Dagger's computer.

The man seemed to have a destination. At the end of the aisle he pulled out a long bin, unsnapped the lid, withdrew something with a long barrel and stuffed it into a duffel bag. "Uh oh. Robber alert." Skizzy dialed Dagger's computer line. "Where the hell ya been?" Skizzy barked.

"In the shower. And I see you have movement." Dagger checked his computer to make sure it was taping.

"Roger that. We've got movement," Skizzy reported, his voice coming through the speakers.

Sara emerged from the kitchen which was emitting fabulous odors. She leaned on the paneled wall and watched.

Einstein was a blur of vibrant colors as he flew over to the perch by Dagger's desk.

"AWK, SHOW TIME."

"Feeling better, huh?" Sara kissed the top of Einstein's head, then turned her attention back to the monitor.

They studied the face of the man, which was partially shielded by the baseball cap and sunglasses. The man hesitated again, this time he seemed to listen for footsteps as he backed around the end of one aisle and waited.

"This could be perfect." Skizzy clicked the mouse directing one of the Micks, the one on the shelf above the man's head, to move. It slowly crawled down the wooden frame and onto the baseball cap. It attached itself to a metal pin on the hat that said *Go Sox.*

Sara asked, "What are you doing, Skizzy?"

"Having fun," he replied with noticeable glee in his voice. "Now wherever our boy goes, Mick follows."

They watched the screen and saw the man leave the Evidence Room in a rush. Once out of eyesight of the surveillance Micks, Skizzy switched cameras where they could watched the scene from the viewpoint of the Mick on the baseball cap. Aisles and doorways bounced in and out of view as the man rushed to the outside parking lot. He approached a brown paneled van with the words *AAA Vending* painted on the side.

"No license plate?" Sara asked.

"Not on the front of the vehicle," Skizzy said. "In Indiana you only have to put one license plate on and it has to be on the rear of the vehicle."

But the picture on the monitor soon jarred and stopped, showing what looked like the floor of the truck.

"Damn," Skizzy muttered. "The guy took the hat off."

"That's okay. He has to put it on or maybe take it with him when he gets home. Just keep recording that monitor but back up the first tape," Dagger said.

The monitor was gray as Skizzy backed up the tape on his end. "Just about ready."

Several seconds later the monitor showed a man in a vendor's uniform and baseball cap looking around the area, then approaching the scanner. He pressed a finger to the scanner and a green light flashed to allow the man access.

Dagger said, "No vendor gains access. Rewind and give me a close-up, Skizzy."

After a pause, the image on the screen showed the man approaching the scanner. The close-up gave a clear picture of the man's finger as it pressed down on another finger, gray and mottled, which he was holding.

"Damn, if Girlie wasn't right," Skizzy's voice sounded over the speaker.

"The name is Sara," she reminded him.

"GIRLIE, GIRLIE," Einstein repeated.

"Great, now you've got Einstein saying it."

"Not exactly *Demolition Man*, but close." Dagger froze the image on the screen and printed several glossy eight-by-tens of the finger being scanned and then the man whose face was shielded by the hat and sunglasses. To Skizzy he said, "Keep an eye on our wayward Mick and let me know if you get any activity."

"Roger," Skizzy said again and clicked off.

Dagger looked at the macaw. "AAA Vending, Einstein."

Einstein cocked his head in thought and soon blurted out, "FIVE FIVE FIVE eight oh eight three. AWK."

"How would he know that?" Sara asked. "Have you ever used them?"

"I never remember what Simon or I may have talked about and only hope the number I need is something Einstein would have in his memory bank." He opened his desk drawer and retrieved a Brazil nut. "Good work." Einstein took his treat and flew back into the aviary.

After calling AAA and catching the owner just before he left for the day, Dagger called Padre to tell him their latest findings.

"Oh, jezzus. That means Lou Riley is dead somewhere. I'll have my men call the bus stations and airports to have their security look for Riley's car. O'Hare is the biggest so we'll start with that one." Padre's sigh was laden with fatigue and frustration. "What the hell is happening? And I don't want to hear about Mercury converging in Pluto's air space or some damn mumbo jumbo."

"Hey," Dagger laughed, "you're the one who sicced the full moon syndrome guy on me. Maybe there's some validity to it, as far as people being crazier than normal." They agreed to meet at AAA in fifteen minutes.

Sara turned off the heat under the chili and brought the pan of corn bread out of the oven. Dagger would be gone for a while and although it was an agreement between them that each eats when they are hungry, not wait for the other person, she wasn't quite hungry yet. But she was curious, curious about the murders.

After checking that the door to the aviary was closed and that the alarm on the front gate was set, Sara ran upstairs and slid open the screen door to the balcony. She closed her eyes briefly and focused on the gray hawk. Instantly she shifted and flew out onto the railing. The sun was warm and the soft breeze riffled through its plummage. It shoved off the railing and took flight.

It climbed fast and headed toward Camden Parkway where the body of Tex Miller had been found. Sara wasn't sure what she would find but the hawk would have a better perspective than the human eye, especially from these heights.

The crime scene area was well-marked, the yellow and black tape like a bright beacon highlighting the gruesome crime scene. The hawk lighted on a tall oak tree, which seemed to be the central point. Sara had heard Dagger and Padre talking on the phone about the case. The grisly details of both the Cambridge and Miller cases coupled with the shape-shifter theory had her mind reeling. Not knowing what to expect and who or what was behind it was intriguing her.

The metallic, pungent odor of blood was carried on the wind, wafting through the branches. Cautiously the hawk made its way down, limb to limb, pausing to search. Sunlight was fading, hovering close to the horizon. There was only an hour's worth of daylight left.

It was obvious where the head of Tex Miller had been impaled. It would take a good rain for nature to rid the stain of death. The scent of blood was becoming too unsettling, so the hawk flew to a large maple tree across the road.

"Not mine." The tall man with ferret features pulled his glasses off and pointed toward the lot. "Add 'um up. I've got twenty-three vans and they are all out there. I service the Northwest Indiana area, lot of government agencies, schools." Eric Volkman had a military buzz cut which was so gray and close-cut he looked bald. He was the owner of AAA Vending in Munster, Indiana.

The van in the picture looked identical to the ones in the lot, same color, same emblem. Padre showed him the picture of the man who had gained access to the Evidence Room.

Eric studied it but shook his head. "He might just as

well wear a mask but what little there is to see doesn't look familiar." He handed the picture back saying, "Ain't hard to get a brown van and paint yellow lettering on it. But Leroy Ambrose has serviced the Cedar Point police and fire departments for the past five years. He's African American." Pointing to the picture, Jerry added, "That ain't Leroy Ambrose."

Dagger looked over his shoulder at Padre and Volkman, then back to the window. He jammed his sunglasses into the pocket of his corduroy shirt and looked down at the waiting area littered with today's papers and empty coffee cups. Ashtrays on two-foot-high chrome stands were filled with cigarette butts and the place reeked of tobacco overload.

Padre asked, "When is the last time you saw Ambrose?"

"Today."

"How many uniforms does each of the drivers get?"

"Three. It's up to them to deposit them in the laundry bin."

"And where is that kept?"

Eric jerked a thumb over his shoulder. "Back room. We use State Line Laundry. Drop off the uniforms every other day. They deliver, like clockwork."

Dagger digested what Volkman had told Padre. No reason not to believe him. The property was secure, surrounded by cyclone fencing and a sliding gate. One thing was certain...the Evidence Room thief wasn't just flying by the seat of his pants. He was methodical and very well-rehearsed.

* * *

The breeze shook the maple tree and although it only weighed two pounds, the hawk felt safer moving down to a sturdier branch. It was at least fifty feet from the crime scene and upwind yet the odor of death was still strong.

A movement caught the hawk's eye and it watched as a ground squirrel scurried for shelter in a hollowed out log. Getting close to dark and it seemed as if the forest's creatures were running for cover. Their instinct's were far greater than a human's. Tex Miller didn't know it wasn't safe to be out after dark.

The metallic odor was not diminishing and the hawk was beginning to wonder if there was a dead animal nearby. It cocked its head, its gaze darting. Shafts of late afternoon sun sprayed bands of sunlight and as the breeze parted the branches, the hawk caught site of the source of the odor.

"What do you think?" Padre asked as he and Dagger walked to their vehicles.

"Check someone in your building. They should be familiar with the regular AAA vendor and immediately question when two show up in the same week. And it might be worth checking out State Line Laundry. Maybe your guy works there, drives the truck."

Dagger?

Dagger's body jerked and he came to an abrupt stop.

You are going to give me...

Sorry. Knock knock, Sara said coyly.

Dagger detected apprehension in Sara's voice.

"Hey? You okay." Padre grabbed his arm to steady him.

"Yeah, fine. My beeper just went off. Wasn't expecting it." This was new to him. Dagger had always been alone before when he and Sara communicated this way. "Hang on a sec."

What's up and what are you doing out this late? Dagger demanded.

Have I got a curfew?

You should. Get home.

First, I think you should know something. After a brief pause, Sara said, *Tex Miller had a passenger.*

Dagger had to think quick—how to talk to Sara and not let Padre know. He checked his beeper as if it were going to show him a number. Then he flipped open the watch face on his wrist which revealed a keypad. It seemed strange to see such a small phone and Dagger wasn't particularly fond of its size but Skizzy wanted him to try it out. Unfortunately, this wasn't one he pressed to his ear. It was all speaker, more like a walkie-talkie. Not something he could use now. So he reached inside the Navigator and pulled out a cellular to dial home, trying to avoid Padre's curious eyes.

Give me the details, he said in thought only.

Sara told him where she was at and how she found the gruesome remains of a woman high on a branch fifty feet from Tex Miller's remains.

Dagger jammed an elbow against the hood of the Navigator and raked a hand through his curly hair. These killings were getting more bizarre by the minute.

"What's up?" Padre's cop nose sensed something amiss.

Dagger slowly pressed the OFF button on the phone. *Promise me you'll go home, Sara. I don't want you out after dark.*

She promised she would leave now.

Turning to Padre, Dagger asked, "Anyone in your office ever locate Miller's wife?"

"Not yet. Why?"

"She may have been riding with him."

17

October 10, 6:10 p.m.

Brian stood over the bed watching Josie sleep. His baseball cap was rolled up in one hand, his duffel bag gripped in the other. The lunch he had prepared for her was still sitting in the tray. She had lost her appetite and that wasn't a good sign. He picked up the tray and quietly left the room.

After depositing the tray on the kitchen counter, he went to his workroom. He tossed the cap on the cot and unzipped the duffel bag. Josie never questioned where he got his money. When he told her he worked for a vending machine company, he wasn't exactly lying. He did wear the employee uniform, he just never reported to work. And he only serviced the area police departments. With the new-fangled security systems they were setting up, he had to get creative. He didn't mean to kill the cop, but he had something he needed—his index finger.

* * *

Within the hour work crews, fire department trucks, lighting, crime techs, and Luther appeared at the third crime scene area. Camden Parkway was again blocked off to traffic. Around the same time a dark blue Buick LaSabre was found in the farthest remote parking lot at O'Hare Airport. The deteriorated remains of Officer Lou Riley, minus one index finger, was found in the trunk. Cause of death was not immediately determined.

Dagger stayed close to his Lincoln Navigator and waited with Padre by the wooden horses since the Crime Lab was using the snorkel again to examine the area where Paula Miller's body had been found.

"How the hell did your informant find out? Even the news helicopters didn't report seeing anything." Padre asked, referring to knowing there was a second rider.

"Trees are still too thick here. My informant," Dagger grinned, "well, let's just say my informant has unique methods. And if you are really patient, I might be able to tell you where the Evidence Room thief lives."

"I don't like it when you have that look on your face." Padre played with the buttons on the Navigator's console.

"What look?"

"I don't know. That look of something sinister and borderline illegal and if I find out too much, you'll kill me."

Dagger laughed. "Nothing sinister. Just one of my bugs from the Evidence Room happened to attach itself to the suspect."

"Are you kidding?"

"No. It's just in a dark place right now so we can't get a good picture. But we will."

"We?" Padre pressed a button and the grid on the dashboard lit up. "What the hell is this?"

"City map."

The console glowed gray and a red blip beeped like a heart monitor.

"What's the red light?"

"Home base," Dagger replied, then turned the monitor off.

Padre played with another latch on his door panel and a gun storage compartment popped open.

"Damn, I gotta get me one of these vehicles."

Surprisingly, very few onlookers were there although several reporters and news crews had heard the report on police scanners and arrived right after the police. Dagger wondered where Sheila was seeing that this might be a big story. The road ahead was lit up like some UFO had just landed, bright light glowing, turning the dark road and forest into daylight. Dagger doubted the killer would show his fangs in this area tonight.

Dagger turned to Padre. "I don't think I'm going to stick around for these festivities. I want to get home and eat dinner while I still have an appetite."

"Don't blame you. But I sure hate getting out of this plushy batmobile."

As Padre placed his hand on the doorknob, Dagger asked, "What about the tapes your man took at the crime scenes? See anyone familiar?"

"There were a couple suspicious looking guys but we

haven't been able to identify any of them." Padre stifled a yawn. "I have to go over to the hotel later and check on Sherlock and Marty. Sherlock is really getting antsy the closer it gets."

"May as well come to my place. They will be there later." After a few beats, Dagger asked, "What's your take on Sherlock, really?"

"If this were the movies, I would say he would be my number one suspect. But this ain't the movies."

Dagger thought about the detailed information Sherlock had on the Addison family and the reams of reports. He turned his gaze to Padre and said, "This isn't exactly real life either."

They were silent for awhile, each lost in his own thoughts, trying to decipher the last thirty hours.

Finally Dagger said, "If, and it's a big IF, Sherlock is right about the killer, then we have to come up with a plan pretty quick. I think Sherlock mentioned the only way to kill it is in its human form and preferably by fire. So put your thinking cap on. We have to come up with a fire-proof structure, like an abandoned concrete building."

"What are you going to use? Napalm?"

Dagger thought about it for a second, mentally going over his cache of weapons in his walk-in vault. "Not a bad idea."

18

October 10, 8:45 p.m.

Caroline Kirby struggled with her purse, laptop, and overnight bag. She felt honored that Sheila would give her a story to write and could see her by-line now. Sheila had asked that she work on it at her penthouse and she would join her after eating dinner at her parents' house.

Just as well. It would give Caroline time to write a preliminary draft of the interview she had conducted earlier with several City Hall workers.

She stared down at the marble floor. The hallway had to be at least ten feet wide and she couldn't begin to estimate how much a penthouse overlooking Lake Michigan cost. Sheila's, according to office gossip, was at least three thousand square feet and cost half a million bucks. Caroline couldn't fathom that kind of money. And now she gets to actually see the place.

There were mailboxes downstairs by the doorman. A doorman. She actually had walked into a building that had a doorman. He had raised his eyebrows at her appearance but Sheila had said to dress casual. Caroline's most comfortable clothes were her torn jeans and UCLA sweatshirt. Her gym shoes were hot pink with matching shoelaces.

She set her overnight bag down and blew a strand of hair from her face. Fumbling with the keys, she finally found the one that fit the top lock. The same one fit the bottom lock. Sheila's father had brought in an expensive designer to decorate her office. Caroline expected no less from the penthouse. The door swung open and she was met with darkness. The drapes were open and sheers billowed in the breeze which sifted through an opened balcony door. The light from the hallway revealed an eggshell-colored carpeting beyond the marble foyer. Caroline closed the door and placed her bags against the wall. Her hand swiped at the wall searching for a switch. With as modern as this place was, she wondered if she had to speak to a computer that controlled all the appliances and lights. She giggled at the thought.

Her eyes detected the image of a lamp on an end table and she moved cautiously toward it. It suddenly dawned on Caroline that she should have asked Sheila if she owned any pets. A dog would have made its presence known by now, but not a cat.

Her hand located the lamp and she fumbled around for the switch. Relieved, she pressed the button several times. Nothing. "Great." She stood and waited for her eyes to adjust to the darkness. Maybe the wall switch was near another doorway.

A long sigh cut through the silence and Caroline

stopped short of stepping further into the room. Was Sheila home? But wouldn't she have turned the lights on? Did she own a fish tank? Room humidifier? Some other appliance that was making that strange hissing sound? Holding her breath, she shut her eyes and opened them, hoping it would make them adjust to the darkness quicker. She strained to listen for sounds.

She felt wisps of hair lift from the back of her head, as if by a cool breeze. Feeling her heart pound in her chest, she tried to convince herself there was a heating vent on the ceiling or perhaps a ceiling fan causing the breeze. Then she felt it again. Instinctively she ran her hand down the back of her head. She never was fond of dark unfamiliar territory and laughed nervously to ease the tension. What happened next literally turned her blood icy—she felt someone's warm breath on the back of her neck and worse yet, she heard the sound of the breath being expelled.

Turning quickly, she stared into a set of eyes so eerie and appalling she couldn't get her vocal cords to respond, to rip out a blood curdling scream. She had heard of people being so frightened they couldn't move much less speak and never believed it was possible. His eyes glowed like smoldering coals and his breath was as hot as an Arizona desert.

She heard someone whimper, a soft cat-like whimper, and realized it was coming from her. Something sharp was pressed against her throat. Slowly it trailed down the front of her. This was not the way she ever pictured herself dying, quivering under someone's power, and she was damned if she was going to let it happen now. With all the strength she could muster, she shoved hard against her attacker and ran for the door. But she no sooner reached the foyer, then he materialized in front of her. Those eerie eyes smiling, a sardonic laugh in his throat. How did he get there so quickly? She turned and ran, bumping against an ottoman, hearing herself scream, feeling herself being pulled down, feeling her fists strike out helplessly. He was too strong. When the fight was all gone, and she felt herself fading, a crazy thought came to her head—who would write her obituary?

Padre pressed his cellular phone to his ear as he lay on Dagger's couch. When he hung up, he announced to the three men, "Luther said Mrs. Miller was probably thrown at impact. Had a fractured skull. Fragments of tree bark in her head match the tree the motorcycle had hit. Died on impact. Lucky thing she wasn't awake when..." His voice trailed off. There was no need to describe in full detail how Paula Miller's body looked like some discarded, dismembered doll some child had cast aside. "I don't understand." He turned to Sherlock. "You said he wasn't brutal until he fully shifted on the thirteenth."

Leaning over his laptop, hands clasped in prayer style, Sherlock paused in thought. Finally, he admitted, "I'm not sure. Maybe it has to do with it being the thirteenth such occurrence. Maybe the accumulation of power over the generations that it/he keeps getting stronger and stronger. I can only assume he won't be fully shifted until the thirteenth. But that doesn't mean his thirst for destruction in human form isn't stronger."

Dagger was sitting at his desk, legs propped on the

corner, hands behind his head. His visitors grew silent. Everyone had declined Dagger's offer of a beer or something stronger, so Sara had made coffee instead. Even Einstein was quiet. Nighttime had fallen and he had taken up his vigil in front of the windows in the aviary. The prescription was working its magic and the macaw was starting to dose off.

Sara stood in front of the aviary watching Einstein. Sherlock was watching her. Dagger couldn't help noticing the gauze tape still wrapped around the professor's hand. Was it admiration in Sherlock's eyes or was he stalking his next victim. Was Simon right? Was Dagger suspicious of any male who cast an admiring glance Sara's way? Or was he just being cautious?

Sara had done something different with her hair. Tiny braids ran down each side of her head. She was trying different things, experimenting, like a curious teenager. He just hoped she wasn't ready to try green hair much less short hair. And how she could go from seeing the gruesome remains of Paula Miller to playing with her hair baffled him. Maybe that was her way of keeping her mind occupied. Any normal eighteen-year-old would have been a basket case. But that was the operative word—normal.

"We're not getting anywhere." Sherlock pulled off his glasses and set them on the coffee table. He stood, clasped his hands behind his head and paced. "What about all those computer searches? I thought you were supposed to be good?" The professor settled his gaze on Dagger.

"Hey," Marty yelled. "We don't need to get on each other's nerves, here."

Dagger nodded toward the stacks of reports on his desk. "If this Addison family has been covering their tracks for two hundred years, what makes you think Paul Addison is going to make it easier for us now?" Dagger thought about what he just said. "Jezzus, two hundred years. Listen to me."

Padre pulled his tie off and tossed it on the coffee table. "I'm just about ready to call in the National Guard and have them comb the forest. That's where he seems to be hanging out."

"Can't do that," Sherlock said. "He'll flee and we'll never find him."

"I agree," Marty said.

"The computer reports are a dead end." Dagger said. "Our guy is too smart to use his real name let alone his real birth date. We don't have the manpower to check every person who moved into Illinois and Northwest Indiana since March of ninety-eight. We have to bring him to us." He searched the faces of the three men. "Any ideas?" A movement by the bar caught his eye. Sara had drifted off to the kitchen and now was pushing open the pass-through. He could almost read her mind. She would be the perfect one to draw Addison's attention. But Dagger didn't want to use Sara as bait. He was supposed to protect her, not hang her out like a piece of meat for the taking.

Dagger moved to the couch and settled on the arm near Padre's feet. Marty was slumped in a chair, Padre was two seconds away from snoring, and they weren't any closer to an answer than the first night Marty and Sherlock showed up on his doorstep.

To Sherlock Dagger said, "There has to be something else in his movement patterns. Does he sleep in a coffin during the day? Frequent new age shops? Steal blood from blood banks? Can't you with all your damn charts come up with anything?"

Padre lifted his hands that were shielding his eyes. "Enough already, you two!" He swung his legs around and sat up. "We're boxing shadows here. I think our main problem is some of us are still in denial and the rest of us seem to have enough belief to carry us all through. Marty, what is it that you said about his mother? What happened in ninety-eight?"

"Paul killed her three years prior and kept her in a bedroom in an isolated farmhouse."

"And your theory on the purpose of that?"

"He had a scapegoat," Marty replied. "She had been the one charged with the murders of her husband and children twenty odd years prior so it was only natural she would be the prime suspect seeing that she had been released a couple years prior to the Purdue murders in ninety-seven. No one knew she was already dead."

"So," Dagger looked at the three men, "where's his scapegoat this time?"

"J.D.," Padre offered.

"That's only good for Lisa's murder." Dagger studied their faces. No one had any suggestions. One by one all their gazes shifted to the clock on the wall.

* * *

Out of curiosity, Sara was at the computer checking the progress of the wayward Mick. Their guests had left an hour ago and Dagger had just retired. The screen showed darkness. It was difficult to tell if the hat was still in the van or if it was lying somewhere in the thief's house. She walked over to the aviary to find Einstein in front of the window again. But this time he was asleep. Dagger had placed the medicine, which he called bird valium, in Einstein's water so he would sleep the night.

After switching off the lights, she trudged upstairs and changed into leggings and a baseball jersey, her latest sleeping attire. She washed her face, brushed her teeth, and tumbled into the cool sheets. Her windows were open several inches to let in fresh air and it was warm and cozy under the cotton blanket.

Sleep surprisingly came easy and within ten minutes she drifted off to a dreamless slumber. She didn't know how long she had been asleep when she was jarred awake. Maybe it was a sound outside, maybe Einstein, maybe Dagger was up. Turning over on her side, she blinked lazily and was just about to drift off when she heard it again.

Saraaaaaaaaaaa.

The sound was long and drawn out and Sara smiled. Why would Dagger be calling her? She heard the sound in her head. Suddenly, Sara bolted to a sitting position. She hadn't shifted so she can't be hearing Dagger's voice.

Saraaaaaaaaaa. Where are you?

It was a sing-song voice, taunting, eerie, sounding as if it were coming from inside her bedroom. But it wasn't. The voice was in her head.

Sara felt her heart pounding against her rib cage and a cold chill swept through her body. She tore out of the room and down the stairs.

Dagger's bedroom door crashed open and it only took him two seconds to reach under the pillow next to him and pull out a Sig Sauer 9mm. The laser sighting fixed a spot of red between Sara's eyes.

There was sheer terror in those eyes and her chest was heaving beneath her baseball jersey. She ran out of the room as quickly as she had run in.

"JEZZUS, SARA. DON'T DO THAT." Dagger fell back against the pillow, his hands shaking as he put the safety back on the gun and buried it under the pillow. What could have spooked her?

He jump out of bed, struggled into his denims and ran after her. He found Sara sitting at the computer, her fingers racing over the keyboard.

"What's wrong?"

She pointed at the computer screen where she had typed:

He's talking to me.

By the absolute fear in her eyes and the trembling in her fingers he knew she wasn't imagining it. But then that would mean Sherlock's theory was correct—there another shape-shifter out there. And he was able to communicate with Sara.

Sara typed:

What do I do?

Dagger realized she was afraid to speak for fear he could hear her.

"Sara?" He grabbed her hands and held them. "Answer him."

Her head shook frantically back and forth.

"Sara." He placed one hand behind the back of her neck. "Sara, listen to me."

Her eyes filled and she blinked away the tears, staring wide-eyed like a child waiting for instructions from a parent, trusting the parent to tell them exactly what to do.

"The only way you can tell if he can hear you talk or hear you mentally is to test it. Now ask him, 'Who are you?'."

Sara took a deep breath to conjure up the courage. "Who are you?" She waited a few seconds.

Saraaaaaaaaaa. I'm waiting for you.

"I don't think he heard me," Sara said. "But he just said he's waiting for me."

"Okay, now I want you to answer him telepathically."

Her eyes, wide as orbs, never left his face.

"You can do it, Honey."

She turned back to the keyboard to type their conversation for Dagger.

Who are you? She said in thought only.

Sara? Is that you?

How do you know my name?

My god, it is you! I saw you today.

Sara swung her head toward Dagger who just motioned for her to keep communicating with him.

Where at?

The animal hospital. I saw what you can do. Are you like me, Sara?

Like you?

"Good, play dumb," Dagger said, reading her typed conversation.

We can be so good together.

I know self defense, nothing more.

I don't think so. I can feel your energy. We belong together, Sara. My sweet, sweet, Saraaaaaa.

"Don't let on that we know his name or anything about him," Dagger cautioned.

You still haven't told me your name.

In time, my sweet Saraaaaa. But I did something for us. You'll be so pleased. Now I have to go. So little time, so many victims.

Sara clamped her hands over her ears as if that would turn him off. She turned to Dagger. "He must have heard us the other night at the warehouse. Maybe he's been listening for years. What if he knows where we live? What if he's outside right now?" Her entire body started to shake and he watched as she ran around the room turning off the ceiling fan light, the light over the bar, the desk lamp.

"Did he stop talking, Sara?"

She shook her head yes as she wedged herself into the corner of the couch and hugged a cushion, her eyes searching the skylights.

Dagger picked up a remote and pointed it toward the wall of windows. He spoke in a calm, logical voice. "He probably can only communicate with you during the time frame Sherlock mentioned, the five days leading up to a full moon. You would have heard from him sooner if it were any different. And if he's like you, he can only hear you when he has shifted or when he's going through this transformation Sherlock mentioned."

Blinds slowly moved downward. Dagger did the same to the kitchen windows and went upstairs and closed Sara's windows. Shafts of moonlight filtered in from the skylights. Then Dagger went into his bedroom, brought out the Sig Sauer and set it on the loveseat. After pulling the coffee table away from the couch, they pulled out the king-sized hide-a-bed. Stumbling in the dark, Dagger retrieved sheets, pillows and a blanket from his bedroom and made up the hide-a-bed. After checking on Einstein who was still snoozing like a baby, he crawled into the bed with his clothes on and opened the blanket for Sara.

"Come on. Talk to me. Tell me all about your grandmother."

She crawled over by him and he held her close. He stroked her corn silk hair. Sara rambled, telling him about growing up on the reservation and her grandparents and life on the road.

She finally drifted off to sleep and he could feel her breathe, her body slowly rising and falling with each breath. He had so easily accepted Sara's unique gift, mainly because he had first-hand knowledge of her shifting and regeneration. If he hadn't witnessed it, though, he might not have been convinced. But if there was another one like her, one with destruction on his mind, why was it so hard for him to believe? Even now, with Sara hearing the killer's voice in her head, he was still not convinced. It could just be Sara's over-active imagination fueled by Sherlock's theory.

But Sara didn't have an over-active imagination. Inquisitive maybe, but she definitely wasn't prone to conjuring up fairy tales.

And one thing was undeniable…Dagger's gut instincts. Something was gnawing at him. Maybe the fact that easy cases just didn't drop into his lap. They were always something a little over the edge, cases clients would be embarrassed to take to your average detective. Probably for fear of being laughed out of the office. And word had gotten around town. Have a relative abducted by aliens? A house being haunted by previous owners? A relative that just won't stay dead? Chase Dagger's your man.

Dagger chuckled in the dark and felt Sara stir, her arm uncurling from under her and stretching across his chest as she settled in closer.

It was going to be difficult to sleep. He could feel every curve of her body and it fit oh so perfectly and felt oh so right.

He stretched on the roof of the high-rise and let the moon bathe him in its energy. It had been so easy to enter the condo of the blonde slut. Crawling up the side of a building was child's play, especially since she left her balcony window open. How stupid to feel so safe ten floors up. Crawling back out and onto the roof was just as elementary.

If only he hadn't lost Dagger and Sara when they had driven from the animal hospital. Lucky for them the gates at a train crossing came down after they passed. He couldn't find Dagger's name in the phone book, not by a last name or a business. Probably wasn't his real name. Probably some macho made-up name like fuckin' Rock or Slade. He'll be taken care of tomorrow and then he'll be able to find Sara. The town wasn't that big and he knew how to reach out and touch her. He laughed at his joke, a sick maniacal laugh that was carried on the wind.

19

Wednesday, October 11, 8:14 a.m.

"What is it, a break-in? That's impossible. Security is tight here." Sheila charged down the marble hallway, spotting Andrea, her cleaning lady seated on a brocade settee, a tissue pressed to her eyes, a police woman kneeling in front of her.

Leyton grabbed his daughter's arm. "Maybe I should go in first."

Two uniformed officers stood like sentinels as they approached. Sheila's heels clicked along the polished floor. Before they reached within ten feet of the doorway, a man in a tailored navy suit and tie, and a pink shirt careened around the corridor carrying a cup of coffee. Hardened criminal came to Sheila's mind. His face was scarred, eyes piercing and unsmiling, dark features. Although he would have scared the daylights out of her in a dark alley, he did have great taste in clothes.

"Miss Monroe?" His voice was emotionless. He may as

well have said, "Hey you."

"Yes, I'm Sheila Monroe." She grabbed her father's arm. "And this is my father, Leyton Monroe."

"I believe the department called you over an hour ago." He was working a piece of gum around his mouth, a slow chew as if there was still flavor left and he was going to savor every last drop.

"I had to shower and wash my hair." Her gold bracelets jangled as she ran a hand though her hair. "What is the problem, Officer..." She looked at his I.D. picture badge. In her years as a reporter, she had interviewed a number of prisoners, and his picture, to her, looked like he should be holding a number under his face.

He glared at her, took a sip of his steaming coffee. "It's Detective Joe Spagnola."

With another glance at his convict-type picture she mumbled, "Why doesn't that surprise me?"

"Sheila, for godsake, will you let the man talk?" Leyton huffed, taking his typical, in-charge stance—chest puffed out, suitcoat open, fists jabbed at his waist, legs apart. A king-of-the-world imitation at its best.

"Why isn't Sergeant Martinez working the case?" Sheila demanded.

"This isn't the dating game. You don't get to pick." The detective led them back down the corridor, away from the penthouse, toward another cushioned settee where he encouraged them to have a seat. "Do you know a Caroline Kirby?"

"She's my," Sheila stopped and sank down onto the plush bench. "Oh, damn. I was supposed to meet her last night to work on a story. I gave her the keys to my penthouse."

"What time did you tell her to arrive?"

Bracelets jangled again as she waved her hands. "Whenever. She was going to go home and pack a bag first since we expected to work into the night. I completely forgot about it and spent the night at my parents' house." Sheila looked down the hall at the sentinels standing guard. "Don't tell me she robbed me blind." With a swirl of platinum hair, she pushed past the detective and stormed down the hall with the two men in pursuit.

"Miss Monroe," Detective Spagnola called out. The men reached the doorway a few seconds after Sheila.

"Oh my god!" Sheila lifted a shaking hand to her mouth as she braced her body against the doorjamb. Leyton gasped and struggled to prop his daughter up.

The living room looked as if someone had held a can of red paint in each hand and spun like a top spraying red from one corner of the room to the other, on the walls, drapes, and furniture. Sprawled in front of the fireplace was the body of Caroline Kirby.

"Oh my god," Sheila cried again. "My new carpeting!"

Leyton released his daughter, letting her drop to her knees. Even he was appalled at her callousness. "For crissake, Sheila. One of our employees has been murdered in your penthouse."

Spagnola casually looked around the room. Years of experience had hardened him to the most gruesome of crime scenes. "To help you put it in perspective, Miss Monroe. At least your furnishings are replaceable."

* * *

Ten thousand for the carpeting, another twenty thousand for the couch, chairs, lamps. Sheila mentally added up the money. Just like some people laugh at funerals or make jokes at the worst of times in an effort to handle the shock, Sheila had her own methods. Nature had eliminated tear ducts from her DNA she had learned a long time ago. Dagger was the only person who could force out a few drops every now and then. And now, to handle the horror of it all, to try to erase the image of Caroline's body, she focused on the furnishings, the replacement value, where she might shop next. Maybe the Merchandise Mart in Chicago. She was making mental lists to avoid the inevitable—the realization that someone had been murdered in her home. How could she ever sleep here again? Now she started to make a mental list of realtors as she twisted her father's hankie. A hand reached out holding a glass of water. She looked up to see Spagnola's unsmiling face.

"Hard, rich bitch. That about cover it?" she said, just as unemotional as he was. She took a sip of water and set the glass down on the marble floor. Spagnola sat next to her, crossed an ankle over one knee revealing socks she knew were only sold at Neiman Marcus. She imagined him being the black sheep of a Sicilian family, the only one who didn't go into the family business but still reaped the cash rewards. It was either cop or thug, cop or thug, eeney-meeney-miney-moe. Now he was snapping the gum like some truck stop waitress.

"Do you know how positively annoying that is?"

After a few more snaps, Spagnola replied, "Yes." He balanced a notepad on his crossed leg and opened it, saying, "People handle grief in various ways. I need to ask you a few questions. I would ask you if you are up to it but being a reporter and being used to sticking microphones in the faces of grieving family members, I'm sure you are definitely up to it."

She leaned back and glared at the detective. "Well, gee, it's a tough business but somebody has to do it." His words stung and now when she didn't want the damn tear ducts to work, they were pumping away like crazy. She pulled out her compact and checked her reflection, dabbed at the dark smudges under her eyes. "What do you want to know? Make it quick because I need to find Caroline's grieving parents so I can torment them." She thought she saw a hint of a smile at the corners of his mouth.

Spagnola read from his notepad. "There was no sign of forced entry so she had to have let the person in. But according to the doorman, there were no pizza deliveries or visitors to your penthouse after Miss Kirby arrived." He turned to face her, mouth chewing slowly. "Who besides your cleaning lady and, I assume your parents, have a key to your penthouse?"

"What are you saying?" Sheila snapped her compact shut. "That someone was waiting in my penthouse for Caroline?"

The detective blinked slowly. "For a reporter, you're not very bright. Someone wasn't waiting for Miss Kirby. The killer was waiting for you. Now again, who else has a key to your penthouse?"

Sheila froze, hoping the shock didn't show on her face.

The only other person who still had a key was Dagger.

20

October 11, 8:58 a.m.

Marty stood in the doorway connecting their two rooms.
The professor was sleeping at the table, his head next to the
laptop, glasses sitting cockeyed on his face. Marty rapped
on the door. "Hey, you going to sleep all day?"

Sherlock jerked to a sitting position and straightened his
glasses. "What time is it?"

Marty stared at the blood stains on Sherlock's shirt.
"What happened?"

The professor rubbed the sleep from his eyes and
noticed the bandage had come off of his hand, the cut bleeding again. "Guess maybe I should have had some stitches."

"Did you get any sleep?"

Pushing away from the table, Sherlock stood and
stretched. "Damn nightmares are coming too often. I
thought I'd work a little on this family tree, see if I could
find something we could use but I keep coming up with
zero."

Marty said, "I spoke with Padre this morning. Want to see the list of homicides from last night?"

"Just give me a number. I don't think I want to know the gory details."

Marty set a copy of the Police Log from the previous night on the table. "Nothing that sounds like him. That's the puzzler. But then he could have picked another town again. After all, he just now started showing up in Cedar Point."

Sherlock picked up the report. "We can't lose him, Marty. He should have felt free to kill now that it's been announced that the boyfriend was arrested for the female cop's murder and the other was still considered a hit and run."

"He's smart, remember." Marty glanced again at Sherlock's bloody hand. "He knows to spread himself thin, not draw too much attention to himself."

"So we need reports from surrounding communities."

"What does your map say?"

Sherlock brought out a bulletin board and propped it on the couch. Pinned to it was a map of a two-hundred-mile radius. For the past two years Marty had obtained figures of homicides occurring on the actual date of a full moon. If any towns reported any violent crimes, he looked at the statistics for the five days prior to see if there was a pattern to the killings. They didn't rule out obvious killings like drug-related or domestic because it would be just like Paul Addison to disguise his handiwork by making it look like an every-day occurrence in a crime-riddled community.

Yellow pins denoted where killings occurred on the date of a full moon. Red pins referred to the homicides occurring one day prior; blue pins for homicides from two to five days prior. A gold pin in Indianapolis reflected the killings from March 13, 1998, the last date of a full moon on a Friday the thirteenth. It was evident by the pins that the killer had definitely moved away from Indianapolis.

"He's going in a circle. See the pattern?" Sherlock pointed to the yellow pins surrounded by blue and red pins.

The map showed clusters. One in Chicago, Evanston, then west of Chicago, South Side of Chicago, and then back across the border to Indiana. According to the dates of the homicides, most had occurred in Illinois. Just recently it started to cluster in Northwest Indiana.

"Provided those are all his doing. But we have no way of knowing. What is it you are looking for?" Marty asked.

"A lair."

"Lair?"

"A home base. He had one in Indianapolis. Remember the farmhouse on the outskirts of Indianapolis?"

Marty nodded. That was where they had found the decomposing body of Paul Addison's mother.

Sherlock took a red marker and drew a circle from Chesterton along the lake shore to the Illinois border just west of Cedar Point and back to Chesterton. "Now we know it's in this area. He could travel just about anywhere. But something is keeping him here for now."

Marty's gaze traveled to the taupe-colored carpeting near the chair Sherlock had slept in, and the drops of blood now dried. "You better have that hand taken care of," he said again.

* * *

"Any movement, Skizzy?" Dagger sat in front of his monitor talking to Skizzy via computer. He heard the heavy clomping of Simon making his way through the kitchen. "Nothing. I think I was able to disconnect the Mick from the pin by disengaging the magnet. The infrared sighting revealed it is in a room, not too large either."

"Padre didn't get any fingerprints off Riley's car." Dagger gave a wave toward Simon and noticed his eagle eyes immediately riveted on the hide-a-bed with its blanket and sheets twisted in knots. "Padre didn't release any information to the press about the theft from the Evidence Room, so we'll keep the Micks in operation in case our guy comes back."

"Will do."

Dagger clicked the mouse to sign off of the phone call. He turned to Simon and quickly pointed a finger. "Don't say a word."

"Not me." The burly postman rocked back and forth on his thick-soled shoes, drew his gaze back to the make-shift bed.

Dagger felt compelled to explain. "Sara was worried about Einstein last night so she slept down here."

"Uh huh, uh huh." His dark eyes twinkled and his thick lips curled up in a smile as he gazed at the Sig Sauer on the loveseat. "And I suppose she was going to shoot him if he didn't behave."

Dagger picked up the Sig and took it to his bedroom. When he returned he glared at Simon saying, "Wipe that smirk off your face. Nothing happened. She's been getting crank calls and she was spooked, that's all." Dagger folded up the blanket and stripped the sheets off the bed.

"Not that you wanted anything to happen." Simon smiled now, a large grin lighting up his face, white teeth gleaming against his dark skin.

"She isn't ready," Dagger finally said.

"She isn't ready?" Simon repeated. "What do you think she is? A three-minute egg?"

Dagger shot a gaze toward the second floor. Sara had gone up to take a shower. With a hefty shove, the hide-a-bed folded in. He tossed the cushions back on the couch.

Simon set Dagger's mail on the corner of his desk. "Well, you better listen closely, because that timer is about to go off in about ten seconds." He chuckled again and lumbered over to the loveseat, plopped his body down. "Heard the latest?"

Dagger grabbed his glass of juice and sat down on the couch, stretching his legs across the coffee table. He shook the sleep from his head and studied the loveable postman. "No, I obviously haven't heard since you're grinning like a damn Cheshire cat."

"That dizzy blonde ex-girlfriend of yours has a dead body in her fancy penthouse."

Dagger slowly pulled his legs off the table.

"Yep," Simon continued, "some co-worker she gave a key to was stabbed to death."

* * *

"Got some good prints here Joe." A chunky man resembling Baby Huey shined a flashlight onto the end table. "Got some on the candy dish, the drawer here, kitchen counter, in the bedroom." Detective Spagnola bent over and pointed with a gloved hand at the candy dish. "Do they belong to Sheila Monroe?"

"We'll know once we get a set of her prints. But there looks to be about four different sets throughout the penthouse. Could be the deceased, Miss Monroe, her cleaning lady, and hopefully, the killer."

Luther watched his staff carry the body of Catherine Kirby across the foyer and out the door. He walked over to Detective Spagnola as he pulled off his gloves. "Multiple stab wounds. Used one of the kitchen knives left at the scene. Wiped clean."

"Time of death?"

"Between nine and midnight."

Spagnola thought for a moment, looked at the items lying by the door. "We can narrow that down even further." He pointed to the suitcase and laptop by the entrance. "Doorman says she entered at around eight-forty. Looks like she never had a chance to set up her laptop or put her overnight bag in the guest room. Maid says none of the lights were on so the deceased never had a chance to hit the switches. Probably didn't know where they were. We can be really specific by saying she was nailed the moment she walked through the door."

21

October 11, 11:05 a.m.

"Good morning, Mr. Dembroski. How are you?" Padre closed the conference room door and walked over to a counter where a coffee maker sat, a full pot sitting in the warming tray. "Coffee?" he asked his guest.

The Hispanic man eyed Sergeant Martinez suspiciously with close-set eyes, low forehead, and teeth with enough space between for an extra set. "Uh, yeah. Black." Fingers with nails dirty and brown-stained, drummed the table absentmindedly. His ferret eyes scanned the room, settling on the mirror behind Padre's chair.

"One black coffee coming up." Padre had a way of disarming suspects with his overly friendly demeanor. He set the coffee in front of the man whose wirey hair looked as if he had lived most of his life under power lines. Padre ran a hand down his tie before sitting down.

"What, no danish?" Manny asked.

"Don't push your luck," Padre replied.

Manny sipped his coffee and nodded his approval. He was the product of a Hispanic bar maid and a Polish shoe salesman. He had spent most of his youth as a runaway, hooking up with a carnival and learning the art of pick-pocketing from gypsies. Most of his arrests had been for petty theft. Whether it was lifting wallets from purses or pants pockets, grabbing necklaces off of unsuspecting train riders, or money out of cash drawers, Manny was one of the best. And he had been arrested three times by Officer Lisa Cambridge.

Although the newspapers ran the story of J.D. being arrested for Lisa's murder, the crime was still being investigated. And Manny's name was one of the perps J.D. had come up with in his search through Lisa's case reports.

"How's it going, Manny?" Padre placed his hands flat on the table. The clean, manicured nails a sharp contrast to Manny's.

"Fine." Manny looked around the sparsely furnished room, his gaze settling on an ashtray near the coffee maker. "Can I smoke?"

"Why sure." Padre pulled out a pack of cigarettes, shook one out for Manny and one for himself. They shared a match and Padre retrieved the ashtray and set it between them.

"Don't think I've ever talked to you before. How come?" Manny took a short drag, like a teenager not used to smoking. He was only in his early twenties but somehow looked older. The carnival had taught him to grow up fast in some ways. In other ways, he should have finished school.

"I work homicide." A slight smile crossed Padre's lips

as he saw the light bulb flicker in Manny's head.

"Homicide? That's like dead people." The young man pushed back from the table. "Whoa. I don't do murders." This time he took a longer drag, picked a piece of tobacco from his bottom lip.

"I know you don't, or at least you haven't in the past." Padre opened a file folder and pulled a pen from his shirt pocket.

"No time, ever. That's one of the ten commandments."

Padre smiled. "So is 'Thou Shalt Not Steal'."

"Unless you're in dire need."

"I must have missed that part of my teachings."

"That's according to Manuel, Chapter Seven, Verse Two." Manny smiled then, his mouth resembling a picket fence.

"Where were you Monday around three-thirty in the morning?"

"Monday?" Manny lifted his head, eyes searching the ceiling, eyebrows scrunched in thought.

Padre knew this was a waste of time. What was done to Lisa took a powerfully strong man and Manny couldn't have weighed more than one hundred and forty pounds soaking wet. But he couldn't rule out the fact that Manny might have hired someone. But could he be that pissed at being arrested for petty theft? Lisa had sent him to prison for a year. He was out on good behavior in three months. Not enough to hold a grudge. J.D. had come up with a short list of possibles. None of Lisa's arrests were serving major time. There were no threats to her in the courtroom by the suspect being dragged away.

"Oh, yeah. I was in church, three-thirty mass." A cocky grin spread across his face. But when Padre reached across the table and grabbed him by the front of his Grateful Dead tee shirt and hauled him halfway across the table, Manny's eyes grew as wide as a child's at Christmas.

"POLICE BRUTALITY, POLICE BRUTALITY," Manny screamed.

"Did you forget the commandment, 'Thou Shalt Not Lie?' You can burn in hell, Manny. But before you get there, I get my ten minutes with you." Padre tightened his grip for several seconds while the skinny guy squinted as if preparing for the deadly blow. Padre released him and Manny sank back against the wooden slats of the chair.

"I was asleep, okay?" He straightened his shirt, moved his shoulders back and forth, making sure all his body parts were still intact. "I picked up a girl at Chico's Bar. She spent the night and no, I don't know her name other than Butterfly."

"Butterfly?" Could only be a hooker, Padre thought. "How much did you pay her?"

Manny seemed to chew that one a bit, hang his head. "Twenty bucks. You think a guy with my looks is gonna get a self-respecting girl? No, I gotta pay. But she was nice, you know? Didn't make fun of my looks, much less my name." He took another sip of his coffee, long drag off the cigarette before smashing the butt into the ashtray.

"When is the last time you saw Officer Lisa Cambridge?"

Manny stared for several seconds at the mirror behind Padre, cocked his head. "This what it's about? I thought they caught the killer."

"May have had help."

"Help? You see the size of that dude?" He finished his coffee and dumped the contents of the ashtray into it. Even swept ashes off the table into the cup. Padre half expected him to offer to vacuum. "No. I have never killed anyone in my life." He placed his hand on an imaginary bible and raised the other. "As God is my witness."

"Well, that was enlightening." Chief Wozniak entered Padre's office having witnessed the interview with Manny from behind the two-way mirror.

"As much as we would like to find a logical killer, we have just about exhausted our list of logical suspects." Padre tossed Manny's case folder on the desk. "I can understand your hesitancy to believe Sergeant Flynn and Professor Sherlock, but right now everything is pointing to an illogical suspect."

Wozniak sank into the chair in front of Padre's desk. "The department put out a press release asking if anyone was driving on Camden Parkway that night but no one has come forward."

Padre hung his suit coat on the back of his chair. There weren't any plaques on his walls or anniversary paperweights on his desk. He personally didn't like those little snippets of 'atta boys' or self-boasting trivia. That wasn't him. He sat down and leaned back, hands clasped across his waist.

"I don't have to tell you," Wozniak started, "that Lisa's

murder is top priority. I can't let J.D. stew for too long. Alderman Siler is screaming racism already. Once she gets her people behind her, she'll have this town in turmoil."

"Let's not forget Lou Riley."

"No, Lou was a good guy. Couldn't wait for retirement. Did you investigate that State Line Laundry?"

"All the employees check out. My guess is Riley's killer stole one of the uniforms. The laundry admits if some are torn and irreparable, they just toss them."

"At least we know there wasn't anything wrong with that new scanner system. It was human error. The night shift clerk actually believed AAA had moved our deliveries to six o'clock. Never double-checked with the day shift."

"Don't you think two weeks off was a little harsh?"

"She should have been fired. Lets a vendor in with a wave, no verification of I.D. And now we have one dead officer. Could have been avoided, Martinez."

Padre spent his lunch time visiting J.D. The young cop was sitting on the floor with the Doberman in his lap. Max's chin was on J.D.'s knee and he was accepting the neck scratching with mild interest.

"How's he doing?" Padre asked.

"Better." He leaned closer to the Doberman's ear. "Aren't you, Max? You're doing much better." J.D. slipped Max off of his lap and the dog curled up on the rug, his eyes blinking lazily.

"He still drugged up?"

"A little." J.D. stuck a mitt-sized hand at the sergeant

and they shook. "Anything?"

"Wish I had something to give you." Padre eyed the furnishings in the spacious suite. Subdued colors, a lot of wood, and heavy on the silk plants. He sat down at the table in the kitchenette and accepted a glass of iced tea.

"Those collars didn't look promising to me either," J.D. admitted as he slid onto the seat across from Padre.

There was never a hint of new growth on his head and Padre imagined J.D. shaved his head twice a day to keep it that way.

"I never did thank you."

Padre cast a quizzical glance over the rim of his glass. "For what?" He set the glass down and peered at J.D.

"Not coming at me like I was the number one suspect. Not being quick to judge me. Black dude, white woman. Had to be the nigger."

Padre shook his head. "No. You're a good cop and a decent guy. I knew your Dad. John Senior taught his boys well."

J.D.'s father had been a preacher, founder of the First Ministry of David Church in Cedar Point. The elder Draper had died of a heart attack at the age of fifty-three. The night he died, he had clasped his younger son's hand and told him, "No father could be prouder."

"He taught by example," J.D. replied pensively.

J.D. remained silent and Padre knew he was reminiscing. Padre finished his tea and looked over at the Doberman who seemed at ease in J.D.'s presence, certainly not the image of a dog in the presence of the killer of its master. But then, Padre never suspected J.D. for one second.

He studied the handsome black man seated across from him. His was an agonizing waiting game. To sit and do nothing had to be the worst, especially for a cop. And now Padre had to deliver more bad news. That was the problem with being a seminary dropout. Other cops managed to drop the tough jobs into Padre's lap. "J.D." Padre's voice was soft, understanding, even before the full message crossed his lips. And the look in J.D.'s eyes was that of puzzlement and then the realization that Padre wasn't here just to socialize. Finally, Padre asked, "Did you know Lisa was pregnant?"

"I need to talk to you, Josie."

Josie scooted to a sitting position. "You sound so serious." Her chin length hair was stringy and lifeless. Just washing her hair was a chore.

He pulled a chair up to her bed. "It is." A suitcase was propped against the nightstand. "Remember I told you one day I would tell you a secret?" She nodded. "I don't want you to get upset, okay?" She nodded again. "I am in the witness protection program and I may have to take off at any given moment."

"Brian, I don't understand." She blinked lazily, her mind too fatigued to think straight.

He pointed to the suitcase. "In that briefcase is money. I've been saving it just in case you would need to pick up and run."

"Brian, what do you mean you may have to take off?" She tried to force herself to sit up straighter as she blinked away tears.

"Calm down sweetheart. I can't go into the details just yet." He carefully sat on the bed next to her and held her hand, brushed the matted hair from her forehead. The television and radio were filled with news about the body of the cop found at the airport. As far as he knew, the cameras had been taken out of the Evidence Room, but he can't try to access it any more. Now he wondered how good of a composite picture of him they had. It might be a good time to change his hair color. They know about the finger. And it left him no choice but to be ready to run. Josie would only slow him down.

Brian forced a boyish grin. "I will find you. I promise. The money should last you for quite some time. Just make sure, if there is any time that I don't come home, that you don't hear from me, if I don't call, you take off. Because they will be after you."

"You're scaring me, Brian." She clenched his hand and pulled him closer.

"No, sweetheart. Look at this as an adventure. Do as I say. Promise me?" He kissed her forehead. "Promise?"

Josie nodded.

22

October 11, 1:20 p.m.

The best aerial view maps were in the Building Department. This was Commissioner Roperson's golf day so Dagger was assured of uninterrupted time with the files. The building inspectors were out on job sites so it was just Dagger and Lucy, an auburn-haired, full-figured woman who was an outrageous flirt. Lucy was just putting a final coat of iridescent green polish onto her sculptured nails so she was more than happy to have Dagger help himself to the rolled up city maps.

"You are just a sight for sore eyes, Dagger. Got a new inspector started couple weeks ago, big guy, all muscle. Like those damn info commercials on cable, you know?" She looked up from her painting job to admire Dagger's physique, the muscular forearms pressing against the rolled up sleeves of his black shirt. "Unfortunately, he's got a body by Fisher and brains by Mattel. Know what I mean."

Dagger smiled. "I know a few women like that, too."

"How do you like the color?" She held her hand out for Dagger to see.

The detective winced. "Might need to put my sunglasses on."

"Think so?" She admired her handiwork. "Good, that's the effect I was looking for."

The phone rang and Lucy used a pencil to push the speaker button. "Cedar Point Building Department. May I help you?"

While Lucy instructed the caller what forms to fill out for a request for inspection, Dagger pushed one map to the end of the long conference table and unrolled another. He was looking for unincorporated areas, possibly forest preserves. If they had to kill Sherlock's mythical creature, they needed it to be in some obscure corner, preferably the forest preserves which are closed to the public at sunset.

"What are you searching for, Honey? Maybe I can help?" Lucy offered after finishing the phone call.

"Two things: A resident living in an unincorporated area and locations of forest preserve property."

"Why didn't you say so." She pointed a day-glo nail toward the wall where a metal roll hung. It looked like the rolled up screen used with a projector. "Just pull on one of the tabs. I think the second and fourth ones are unincorporated areas. The fifth shows all the preserve properties."

He had no doubt that the reason the department ran so smoothly was Lucy. After the men in the department left the office in shambles, Lucy didn't leave until everything was put back in its rightful place.

The maps were detailed and current, especially since

heated debates had been going on for the past eight years regarding the location of a third airport for the Chicago and Northwest Indiana area.

Lucy trudged over to where Dagger stood, her floral moo-moo swaying with her hips. He noticed her feet in beach-type flip flops with wads of pink cotton between her toes. Her toe nails had been painted the same green color.

She got up close to him and sniffed. "Damn, you always smell good."

Dagger smiled at the forty-something woman with the auburn hair pinned on top of her head like a Flintstones character.

Lucy blew on her wet nails. "Once these babies are dry, Sweetie, you can have your way with me."

"Why have I been summoned?" Sheila stood in front of Detective Spagnola's desk, fists jammed onto the waistline of her linen suit. The skirt hit mid-thigh and every cop in the room had craned his neck when she walked in.

"Did I interrupt your shopping?" Spagnola grabbed a folder off of his desk and stood. "Follow me."

He led her down a hallway and stood in the doorway to a cramped room. She winced at the tackiness of the marred table and stained carpeting, and was reluctant to sit down in the chair. Pulling a tissue from her purse, she wiped the chair before sitting down.

"I answered all of your questions earlier." She sat down gingerly and wiped the arms of the chair with the same tissue before placing her elbows on it.

Spagnola took a seat across from her and opened up the folder. Pages of notes were clipped to the left side. Without looking up from his notes, he said, "I'm sure those are wear and toss clothes so I don't know why you are concerned with getting your suit dirty."

"I have no idea what pervert was sitting in this chair last." She cocked her head to view the edge of the table and caught him staring at her, a dark scowl forming. "Well, at least you'll be happy to know I didn't hunt down Caroline's parents."

"I'm sure they appreciate that. They will be flying in from Baltimore tonight."

He held up three sets of fingerprints and showed them to her. "Yours, the victim's, and your maid's prints have been confirmed. But there is still a fourth set not yet identified, and these prints were all over the damn place. AFIS didn't come back with anything so our killer seems to be non-existent, or at least he doesn't have a record."

"What makes you think it might be a he? That's pretty sexist, isn't it?" She pulled a cigarette from a gold case and held it up.

Spagnola waited a few seconds, then pulled out a lighter. Her gaze held his and she inhaled deeply. His eyes weren't on her, they were on her left hand.

"I noticed your ring this morning, Miss Monroe. Looks like an engagement ring."

Sheila held her hand out as if wondering how the thing got there. "Oh, this?"

He flipped several pages in his notes. "According to undisclosed sources, you were engaged to a Chase Dagger.

Why didn't you mention him?"

"Am, not were." She took another long drag from her cigarette and let the smoke drift out slowly. "We are very close."

"Close enough to give him a key, I take it?"

"I don't remember. He had one at one time, then left it at my place, then took it again. Hard to keep track."

"Very close," He repeated, leaning back in his seat, his eyes hardened, unmoved by her batting eyelashes and hiked skirt. "He tossed a glossy eight-by-ten at her. Someone had snapped a picture yesterday near the scene of the hit-and-run. In the photo Dagger was jabbing a finger in the air toward her and both of their mouths were open in what looked to be an unfriendly exchange.

"My occupation sometimes gets in the way," she replied simply, tossing the picture back at him.

Spagnola made a cursory examination of the man in black, dark eyes, long hair, earring. A man that size could very easily overpower a woman. But the victim hadn't been overpowered. She had been surprised and just about any size person could have done it.

"Who would want to see you dead, Miss Monroe?" He fondled the photo now, turning it, spinning it slowly to face her and back toward him. "I'm sure your investigative work might have pissed off quite a few people." He watched her gaze rest on the photo, a look of forlorn, or was it longing, in her eyes. "Do you know the percentage of homicides that are crimes of passion?"

"Dagger would never harm me. He loves me." Her eyes flashed and she tilted her chin in defiance. "There is one person who has access to Dagger's set of my keys. And she definitely isn't fond of me."

While Sheila was left smoking her pack of cigarettes in one of the conference rooms, two patrolmen were escorting Sara through the doorway. The men in the room were getting whiplash. First it was the classy blonde, now a young woman with waist length hair, skin like porcelain, and exotic eyes that seemed to glow like turquoise gems. No flashy clothes or jewelry. Just down-to-earth corduroys, cropped yellow sweater and a cropped leather jacket the color of butter.

If Spagnola thought Sheila's eyes flashed defiance, this one's were downright hostile.

"Miss Morningsky?" Spagnola held out a chair but the young woman stood her ground.

"What is the meaning of this?"

"Is the Crime Unit doing a thorough search of the property?" Spagnola asked one of the uniformed officers.

"We couldn't get on the property," he replied.

"What?" Spagnola turned to Sara.

"That is reservation property. Your search warrants are worthless." When it came to protecting her home, Einstein, and Dagger, Sara was an absolute pit bull.

"Well, well." Spagnola hung one hip on a corner of his desk. "Didn't know the address we had was reservation land. My apologies." He pointed to the chair. "Please sit. I just have a few questions."

Sara looked at the chair but remained standing. "Where

is Sergeant Martinez?"

"Busy." He had to smile. No wonder Sheila Monroe was an ex-fiancee. Sara Morningsky looked ready and willing to fight for her man. Question was: Just how far was she willing to go?

"What is this about?"

"A murder."

Sara wondered why she would be called in. Had Padre mentioned her name during any conversations regarding the strange homicides lately? How could she possibly help? She waited, stared blankly at him until he offered more information.

"Do you know Sheila Monroe?"

She had heard about the murder in Sheila's penthouse. Dagger told her about it this morning.

"She is my..." she searched for the right word, "associate's ex-fiancee."

"Associate?" Spagnola smiled.

Sara heard chuckling behind her and her eyes darted to the faces at the desks. Although it wasn't like shopping at a crowded mall, she was still around strangers, standing alone, all eyes on her. She was supposed to feel safe in a police station but for some reason she felt like the accused.

All she could think of to say was what she had heard people say on television. "I would like to speak to my attorney."

23

October 11, 2:55 p.m.

Spagnola watched the two women's reactions as Sheila was led into the squad room. He didn't know where the term green with envy came from. If jealousy had a color, it had to be fire engine red. Flames seemed to be shooting from Sheila's eyes.

But the younger girl was passive, no flames there. Indifferent or confident would be a better word. According to Sheila, Chase Dagger lived and worked in the same house with the young, downright gorgeous woman. If looks could kill, he would have another homicide on his hands right in front of his desk.

"Well, did you arrest her?" Sheila demanded, marching up to Spagnola's desk, her eyes glaring at Sara. "Take her fingerprints?"

Sara looked at her hands, wondering if something she touched here might have had a sensor that already had her prints in some database somewhere. Skizzy had a way of making even her second-guess the authority. Instinctively she balled her hands into fists, half expecting someone to pull her hand over to a black ink pad. The double doors to the room burst open and Dagger charged in. Hell and spit-fire dressed in black from head to toe, swept in on a dark cloud that had cops edging back, hands reaching for their weapons.

He was an impressive figure in a long black trench coat, not what Spagnola had expected. Usually some short shit guy with baby face good looks, or someone ugly as sin but dripping in money have women fighting over them. But this guy filled the doorway, not fat, but tall and solid, an edge of danger, the kind that casts a shadow and makes you move out of his way.

Spagnola watched the mysterious man enter. Unlisted in any telephone directory. Little odd for someone running a business. No rap sheet, no fingerprint record. Another odd tidbit seeing that he used to be a Marine and attended the police academy. Chase Dagger's eyes, cold and accusing, riveted on Spagnola and the cop felt the hint of a chill up his spine. Then Dagger's eyes jerked to Sara.

"Are you all right?"

Sheila ran to him, flinging her arms around his neck. "No, Sweetheart. It's been awful." She clung to him, but may as well have been hugging a piece of plywood. He didn't even wrap a consoling arm around her, just kept staring at Sara.

"They want my fingerprints," Sara said.

"What?" He pushed Sheila away and crossed the distance to Sara in three long strides, then leveled a glare at

Spagnola. "What's going on?"

Spagnola moved to the chair behind his desk.

"I didn't want to tell him you still had a key to my place, but he forced it out of me," Sheila said.

Dagger looked from Sheila to Spagnola. He glared and waited, hands jammed at his waist.

"You're a hard man to pin down, Mr…" Spagnola checked his notes. "Is it Charles Dagger?"

Skizzy had filled the database with sketchy information on him so Dagger wasn't too worried about what the cops did or didn't know.

"No," Dagger replied, offering little else.

"We need yours and Miss Morningsky's fingerprints."

"Why? She's not involved," Dagger said, tossing a nod toward Sara. "I was just at Sheila's place a couple days ago. Of course my prints would be there."

Sheila grabbed his arm. "And that's what I told him."

"No you didn't," Spagnola countered. "All you said was that Miss Morningsky had access to your boyfriend's keys."

Dagger turned on Sheila, he wanted to grab her and shake her. She could do whatever she wanted to him but once too often Sheila had targeted Sara. "You have crossed the line, this time."

"You have no idea what she is capable of." Sheila argued. She peered around him, pointing. "Look at her, all smug, knowing you'll come to her rescue. She could probably slit your throat while you're sleep…"

Dagger grabbed her. "STOP IT!" He wanted to squeeze the living life out of her but suddenly realized this was what the cop wanted. Provoke them into a fight. He released his grip and looked at the smug grin on the cop's face. "Have any doubts now why she is an EX-fiancee?"

He grabbed Sara's hand. "Come on, we're getting out of here."

"No you aren't." Spagnola stood. Showdown.

Padre barged into the room. "What's going on here?"

"Not your case, Martinez." Spagnola had had his own share of run-ins with Padre. Padre was from the old school of police work. Spagnola liked to cut corners, get to the truth no matter what methods.

Padre looked at Sheila and Sara and it didn't take him long to size up the situation once he remembered the homicide earlier in the day at Sheila's penthouse.

"Chief and I need to talk to Dagger."

"I'm interrogating him and his..." he grinned at Sara... "associate. Need to send them both down for printing."

"Well, if either of them are suspects, you better take my prints, too. Because on more than one occasion I have wanted to kill Miss Monroe myself."

Dagger squeezed Sara's hand. "Come on."

Spagnola barked, "She stays."

"Over my dead body."

Sheila watched them leave, those tear ducts starting to pump. "Are you going to let them leave?"

Spagnola sighed. "I know where to find them."

"Thanks for the rescue," Dagger told Padre.

"You owe me one." Padre escorted them from the building. Chief Wozniak didn't need to see Dagger. It was just

Padre's way of getting Dagger out from under Spagnola's eagle eye.

Dagger told him about the maps in the Building Department and how he had found a couple good possibilities for fire-proof structures. "While I was there I also obtained a list of residents living in unincorporated areas. Not that our suspect is using his real name. Never know if one of the names might jog Sherlock's memory."

"Why don't we go look at those structures? I'll call Marty and we can swing by and pick him up. Sherlock is supposedly napping. That guy stays up all night and naps during the day."

Dagger stopped short of his truck, which Sara had driven to the police department. She had refused the police escort to the station and instead insisted on driving herself.

"I'm going to go home," Sara said.

"Sure?" Dagger held the truck door open and she climbed in. "You okay after...? He tossed a nod toward the police station.

Sara smiled. "I'm fine. But I don't understand why Sheila hates me. I haven't given her any reason."

"With women like Sheila, there doesn't have to be a reason," Padre said. "She's possessive and hard of hearing."

"Hard of hearing?" Sara said.

"Yeah," Padre chuckled. "Doesn't quite hear the phrase, *'not interested'*."

* * *

Sherlock heard someone say "room service." He hadn't called room service. He stuck his glasses back on his nose and pulled the door open.

"I'm sorry, I didn't order anything."

The waiter smiled. "Your neighbor was afraid you were going to forget to eat."

Sherlock smiled at Marty's thoughtfulness. He had been too busy to bother with lunch and had thought about going down to the restaurant. But the aromas coming from the chafing dishes were enticing. He moved several stacks of papers away and watched as the waiter set the three plates, wine glass, and wine chiller on the table. A bottle of white zinfandel was buried under a mass of ice. The waiter uncorked the wine and filled his glass. Sherlock handed the man five dollars and closed the door behind him.

He didn't realize how hungry he was until he lifted the chafing dish and saw the size of the steak. Under the second chafing dish was a baked potato and green beans. Under the third was a loaf of bread.

"Thank you, Marty." Sherlock took a swallow of wine and sat down to his early dinner.

24

October 11, 6:10 p.m.

Marty opened the door to his hotel room and switched on the lights.

"Refrigerator is behind the counter. Help yourself to something cold. But don't…"

"I know, I know," Padre said with a wave of his hand. "No alcohol. Gotta keep a straight head."

Dagger parted the drapes and peered out into the haze. Dusk was fast approaching. Another night and they were no closer to finding Paul Addison. Drawing the drapes open, he said, "I think the structure we found off Tower Road will work just fine." Tower Road was an unused gravel road leading deep into Beacon Preserve, a forest preserve south of I-80 and near the quarry. There weren't any parks or picnic groves and the most isolated site they had found.

Padre twisted off the cap and took a swallow of juice. "Now all we gotta do is lure the guy there. Going to be hard when no one seen much less talked to him."

Dagger looked away from his friend. How could he tell Padre that Sara had heard from Paul Addison without him wondering how? "If he was in the crowd at the crime scene areas and if he's done his homework, then I'm sure he already knows who we are."

Marty shuddered. "That's a comforting thought." He stripped out of his shirt and tossed it on the bed.

"Getting all dolled up for Sara?" Padre joked as the Indy cop washed up in the bathroom.

"I've been in the same damn shirt all day and it's sticking to me." He struggled into a clean undershirt and a blue pullover. Wetting his hands, he patted down the stray hairs on the sides of his head.

"If you put on aftershave, we'll know you aren't getting dolled up for us." Padre swallowed the last of his juice and tossed the bottle in the garbage.

Marty's face flushed as he walked to the adjoining door. "Sherlock better not be sleeping." He pulled open the door and peered inside. "Yo, Doc. You up?" He took a tentative step into the room. "Looks like he already ate." Remnants of food littered the plates on the table. Stacks of papers had been moved to the side next to the laptop, its screen dark.

Padre lifted up the half empty bottle of wine. "Thought we were keeping a clear head?"

Dagger pointed toward the bathroom door which was ajar. "Someone else is probably primping for Sara."

Marty rapped his knuckles against the door. "Hey, Doc. We're going over to Dagger's house to talk about the final hour. You coming?"

No answer.

Marty looked back at Padre and Dagger, then back to the door. "HEY. Fall asleep on the can?" He rapped again, letting his knuckles push the door open. He wasn't prepared for the scene before him. "Oh, jeez, Doc."

Marty sat on the bed in Sherlock's hotel room, his face pale, eyes cast down. He had found Sherlock's nude body lying in a tub of bloody water. The professor had used the steak knife to slit his wrists.

"I still can't believe it." Marty kept shaking his head. "I worked with the guy for over two years."

Padre squeezed Marty's shoulder. "But it all makes sense now, doesn't it? How he knew so much about the killer, the history of the murders. It isn't uncommon in psychological cases that the killer blocks out the actual events and denies any involvement."

"But what about Paul Addison? My god, we were sure we had the right guy." Marty's gaze drifted to the bathroom where he could hear the medical examiner's instructions to his staff on removing Sherlock's body.

"He did a good job of throwing everyone off track."

Dagger stared at the laptop where Sherlock had typed a two-sentence confession:

I killed them all
I have to stop myself

Could Sherlock have really created such an elaborate history to make it seem as if there were some uncontrollable evil from 1800? And so convincingly that he would have the police believe him?

"Well, at least we can release J.D. now," Padre said. "I never fully believed that shape-shifting shit anyway." He squeezed Marty's shoulder again. "Don't blame yourself for not seeing it. Hell, he had Dagger almost convinced and that's a hard thing to do." He sat down next to Marty and they watched as the gurney carrying Professor Sherlock was wheeled out of the room. "I've seen it before. Killers are so out of it that they convince themselves that someone else is doing the killings. And how many times has the killer been part of a community group helping the police?"

Marty just stared, wiped his eyes. "Guy was like a son to me. I got to know him pretty good the past two-and-a-half years. I just..." He hung his head and stared at his hands.

Padre looked at the stacks of reports Sherlock had labored over. "I don't suppose you want to keep any of this?" Marty shook his head no. "Does he have next of kin?" Marty shook his head again.

"I'd like to take them," Dagger said. He located Sherlock's briefcase and stuffed the reports inside, then placed the laptop in its carry case. "Why don't we go back to my place. I think we can all do with a beer now."

"I still don't believe it." Sara hugged herself. She wasn't sure whether to be elated it was over with, no more voices in her head, or sad because Professor Sherlock was dead. "He was so nice."

"So was Ted Bundy." Padre dipped the bread into his chili and shoved it in his mouth.

They sat around the kitchen table. Marty plunged his spoon into his bowl, finding it difficult to get anything but the beer to go down. The bread was warm and oozing with butter and although it smelled of herbs and cheese, it had no taste. Nothing had taste, not even the beer. It was as if all of his senses were on shutdown.

"Do you know how many deaths might have been prevented if I just had my eyes open?" Marty took a pull on his beer bottle. "I'm definitely retiring when I get back home. Every time I close my eyes, I'm going to see the faces of all those victims."

"He had us all fooled, Marty. Guy comes in here like an authority figure, we should have sensed something was up." Padre looked to Dagger for help.

"He was clever," Dagger offered. "To be able to get that cop's body and the motorcyclists up in those trees." He watched Sara pick at her crab meat salad. Every now and then her eyes would dart toward the windows to search the darkened yard. She probably wouldn't be convinced until she could spend the night without the killer contacting her.

By ten o'clock they poured Marty into the front seat of Padre's car and sent them on their way. Dagger watched the monitor to make sure the gate closed and locked, then set the alarm and settled down on the couch. Sherlock had done a lot of research on the Addison case and Dagger was curious how much material he might have on shape-shifters.

He started sifting through the reports, surprised at the detail. The first report he read was on the origin of

Halloween and how it was started with the Celts. The god of death was some idiot by the name of Samhain. The Celts believed that ghosts and spirits, some evil, roamed the earth on October 31. So they built huge fires and wore disguises to scare off the evil spirits. Druids, a name Dagger had often heard in relation to Halloween, were actually Celtic priests, and they sometimes offered sacrifices to Samhain. Druids also performed magic and with the clash between the beliefs of Christians and Celtics, it wasn't surprising that ghosts, witches, black cats and other weird things became symbols of Halloween.

Dagger wondered if this was how Sherlock fabricated the ancestry of the Addison family tree, that it all started with Henry Addison being feared a warlock. How many years did it take for Sherlock to concoct this fantasy explanation? And he could have shaken just about any family tree to come up with a history of witchcraft. So why Addison? He was local and convenient?

The dishwasher hummed in the background and he saw the light click off in the kitchen. "Going out?" Dagger asked as Sara walked over to his desk.

She shook her head and looked out through the large plate glass window at the moon looming overhead, just thirty hours shy of being completely full. "I think I'll feel more comfortable going out after October fourteenth."

"Know what you mean. This entire case has given a lot of people the willies."

Sara sat down at Dagger's desk and touched the mouse. The screen came alive. A three-inch square in the upper right hand side was dark gray. "Guess Skizzy hasn't been able to move Mick from under the hat."

"No, but he's working on it. The audio detected something but the thief hasn't picked up or moved his hat."

Dagger's eyes caught a page in Sherlock's stack on Shimmers. Supposedly just like shape-shifters but they transform into alien creatures. Dagger chuckled as he read about people who straddle different dimensions and how their physical beings bleed through from one dimension to another. The pages looked like information Sherlock printed off of a web site on alternative life forms.

An extreme close-up of the Manitou, a vicious, wolf-like humanoid from Native American folklore. The concept of a man transforming into a beast-man can be found in all cultures. The monstrous, towering Manitou lurks in the shadows of a cabin. Man-animal related murders predate the oldest X-File by 150 years; members of the Lewis and Clark expedition wrote of Indian men who could change their shape into that of a wolf.

This from a trading cards database. Sherlock had been a very busy man elaborating this farce. Dagger pulled a sheet on lunar phases onto his lap and leaned back to read it.

Scientific research shows no causal factor between the full moon and abnormal behavior, although people who work in state mental hospitals do notice an increase in anxiety among its patients. There are more calls to telephone crisis centers and more babies are born around the time of the full moon.

Dagger chuckled again trying to correlate a water bag breaking to the lunar gravitational pull.

However, although science doesn't support the lunar effects, people do believe it. Psychiatric nurses and emergency room technicians see a noticeable increase in the number of people admitted. Close to eighty percent believe the full moon affects people's behavior.

Dagger watched Sara. She had been standing in front of the aviary door for the past five minutes. Slowly she moved over to the wall of plate glass windows and looked out into the moonlit yard. To the casual observer, the moon looked full. According to Sherlock's notes, the moon officially is considered full for only three minutes.

Another report on shape-shifting caught Dagger's attention. Sherlock had scribbled notes in the margin: *bear, fox, leopard, seal, tiger, wolf.* Were these the only animal forms people could shift into according to these bizarre web sites? Or were they what Sherlock wanted to believe? Dagger looked at Sara and wondering why Sherlock hadn't listed a hawk. And what about the falcon or whatever bird Marty claimed left feathers at the murder sites back in 1998?

According to Sherlock's notes, there were advantages to shifting between forms.

The transformation doesn't include any of the shifter's equipment or clothing. A shape-shifter in animal form can communicate with other members of its species but cannot

speak or use social skills. In human form, the shifter pos-
sesses all the characteristics of a normal human but does
vaguely resemble features of its animal form.

Dagger again looked over at Sara. The hawk and the
wolf both possess her dazzling turquoise eyes. And her hair
in its multitude of colors resembles the coat of the wolf and
the feathers of the hawk.

He lifted the beer bottle to his mouth and slowly took a
sip, his eyes trained on the papers. The report delved into
some deep subjects talking about physical and astral planes.
Then his eyes caught the word regeneration.

A shape-shifter loses all special regenerative powers
when in human form.

That wasn't true, Dagger thought. He had watched Sara
regenerate in human form. Maybe it is faster in animal form.
He read on.

Massive tissue injury such as burning, can result in the
death of a shape-shifter. A shape-shifter is virtually immune
from death in animal form.

Dagger smiled at the paragraph on silver allergies. The
mere touch of the metal causes burn-like welts. Dagger con-
jured up in his mind the old wolfman movies where the
beast can only be killed with a silver bullet.

Turning the page, he read about automatic shifting, primal forms, and blood shape-shifting. "Where the hell did

you find all this?" Dagger whispered. Sherlock must have worked half his life digging up information and inventing a fabulous tale but why something so utterly unbelievable just to cover up his serial killer tendancies.

He took another swallow of beer, kicked his shoes off and dragged his legs onto the coffee table. As he read, he realized there had to be others out there just as strange as Sherlock to have even put this stuff on the Internet.

But a part of him was finding validity in what he was reading, especially the part about automatic shape-shifting. The body can shift automatically when in danger. He thought of the instance in one of their previous cases where a suspect was attempting to rape Sara. She shifted instantly, not caring that the man would witness her shifting.

He read on. It said if the shifter is drowning, the body will shut down, allow itself time to shift into an aquatic form. According to the report, the primal form was the most vicious. It is more bestial in nature, out of control, and can constantly change to adapt to its threat.

Blood and demonic shifters can imitate anyone they want. They have the ability to duplicate internal organs providing extra eyes or limbs. They can grow wings, gills, scales, talons, without having to shift into a specific form. They can also be in psychic contact with others.

A shudder ran through Dagger's body. This sounded like something out of a sci-fi movie. Although he couldn't deny Sara's ability, he still found it hard to believe there was anyone else like her, or someone as vicious as these reports implied. But then...

"Sara." When she turned from the window, Dagger asked, "Are you sure you heard someone talking to you last night?"

"Yes, positive." She walked toward him. "Why?"

Dagger set the report down and studied the young woman. She was childlike in some ways but was far from a gitty teenager, didn't exaggerate, and sometimes was more analytical in her thinking than he was.

"We're all trying to dismiss Sherlock as some serial killer and nothing metaphysical. But how does that explain how he communicated with you?"

Slowly, Sara sank onto the loveseat, their gaze locked. She seemed to mull the question over in her mind and with a subtle shrug admitted, "I don't know."

25

Thursday, October 12, 7:30 a.m.

"No missing persons, no one dancing in the moonlight, no homicides. Very quiet night," Padre reported. "Couple fights at a local bar, few family disturbances, but that's it."

"Guess that should make us rest easy." Dagger cradled the phone between his ear and shoulder as he poured water into the coffee maker and pushed the START button.

"You don't sound convinced."

Dagger told him about some of the reports he had read last night. "Sherlock did some major research."

"Might have been a thesis in college he had worked on. Some people latch onto a hobby and don't let go."

"I didn't notice too in-depth a report on Sherlock's death."

"Other than reporting that he confessed to the slayings prior to taking his own life, I didn't want to reveal any of his sick theories and I just hope the press doesn't catch wind of them either."

"Luther do an autopsy yet?"

"Yes. No water in the lungs. Went down just as we witnessed. He'll place a rush on the toxicology report."

"What's Marty doing today?"

"Probably still sleeping off a hangover. I told him to give me a call when he wakes up. What about you?"

Dagger walked out onto the back patio and stretched, inhaled the morning air. The ground was covered in a sheen of dew and a low haze clung to the deep thicket of underbrush in the distance. "I'm just waiting for a little activity on my one bug that followed our thief home and then we can wrap up the Evidence Room case. What about the Caroline Kirby case?"

"Her parents are going to stop by today to I.D. the body. Such a shame."

"Any suspects?"

"Other than you and Sara?" Padra laughed. "Spagnola is waiting on all the forensics reports to come in. The victim wasn't raped. Killer had to have a key. Only way to get in the place unless he flew in."

Another shudder ran through Dagger's body. He checked on the coffee. "I don't want to hear about any killer flying, climbing trees, or doing any other strange things."

"Well, be prepared. Spagnola's got his sights set on you. Just give me a call if he gets overbearing. You have an alibi. We were all with you that night. And we were all with Sara."

Dagger hung up and poured himself a cup of coffee. He unfolded the morning paper and sat down at the kitchen table. The front page screamed tabloid headlines. Sheila managed to get her face prominently featured in a distraught yet planned pose. His fingers gripped the cup as he skimmed through her interview which she sprinkled with all kinds of inuendos about the killer being someone who had it out for her, that Caroline was not the target. Even Dagger's name had been brought up to which Sheila had supported her fiancee one hundred percent. "He is just as distraught as I am," Sheila was quoted as saying. A couple times Sheila slipped, although he doubted it was a slip up, and referred to the killer as a she.

For some reason, lately, whenever he thought of Sheila, his thoughts drifted to the movie *Play Misty For Me* which was about a DJ who was being stalked by a one-night stand.

Dagger answered the phone on the first ring. He was sorry he did.

"Dagger, Honey. Did you see the papers?"

"You practically all but spit out Sara's name in the article. What do you want, Sheila?"

A cool breeze drifted in from the jalousie windows behind the sink. Dagger got up to close them and watched a light sprinkle dot the concrete patio.

"I have to find a new place to live. I just can't return to my penthouse. As long as I have to do that, I thought maybe we could look for a place together."

Dagger laughed. It wasn't sinister or vicious. He was actually amused. "I don't know, Sheila. Why don't you just come here and live with Sara and me until you have a new place built?"

Silence. Then Sheila blurted, "You're being funny, right?"

"Actually, you can live here and take care of Einstein

since Sara and I will be in prison."

Sara stopped in the doorway, cocked her head as though she didn't hear correctly. One perfectly formed eyebrow jerked up.

"You made it perfectly clear in the article, Sheila, that either one of us did it. Matter of fact, it was a conspiracy. We planned it together. How's that for headlines?" Dagger pushed the END button.

"Sheila?" Sara asked as she grabbed the carafe.

"You're changing from a tea to a coffee drinker."

"Thanks to this case. I kept tossing and turning. Not sure if I was relieved no one tried talking to me or nervous that someone would."

He held his cup out for her to fill. "Sherlock left us all with frayed nerves. Read any of those reports he had?"

"Can't believe what floats around the Internet. I never heard of astral perception or limited, primal, blood shape-shifting. It almost sounds cartoonish." She curled her jean-clad legs under her and sat across from Dagger. Her hair drifted down her arms, captured in the folds of the oversized pullover. Her eyes caught the headline.

"What did she want?" Sara asked, referring to the phone call from Sheila.

"Poor thing can't ever return to her filthy penthouse so she's looking for another one and wanted me to find something we can both live in." He shoved the sleeves up on his black Henley, pulled his hair behind his ears. He glanced at his partner. Sara had been hurt on more than one occasion by Sheila and he wondered how much longer she would put up with it.

"Why did you say we were both going to be in prison?" She crooked her head to see the paper and Dagger pushed it toward her.

"She basically insinuated she knew who the killer might be and all but named you."

Sara didn't smile, just nibbled on her bottom lip as she read the interview with Sheila. If she had any opinions, she wasn't sharing.

"How about an omelet?" Dagger rose from the table.

The young woman smiled. "You're cooking?"

"Sure. One vegetable omelet and one with artery clogging sausage coming right up."

"You must really feel guilty about Sheila's article."

Dagger shrugged, dragged ingredients from the refrigerator and a fry pan from the cabinet. "I thought I left that baggage at the curb when I moved here. You shouldn't have to deal with it."

"Does that mean you'll visit me in prison?"

He wasn't sure if she was kidding or not. Her face was buried in the papers and he couldn't see those expressive eyes that revealed her slightest mood.

Sara kept skimming the papers. But a small obscure headline on the bottom right-hand side of Page 6 escaped her and even Dagger's attention. It read:

Farmers Report Numerous Cattle Mutilations
in Hebron, Indiana

26

October 12, 9:10 a.m.

"Hello, Mr. Burglar." Skizzy dragged the pointer on the screen to the control panel and enlarged the image on the monitor. He had moved the Mick last night once he was sure it had freed itself from the hat. Now the thermal sighting lens enabled Skizzy to observe the windowless narrow room.

Several hand guns rested in a rack hanging on the far wall. Mick slowly panned another wall, vacant, except for a cot, and near the far end, a latch-type opening closer toward the ceiling. Skizzy estimated the room to be about seven feet high, maybe less. Was this some type of delivery door? A full length door was on the opposite wall and Skizzy could only guess this doorway led to the rest of the building. Maybe it was a house, maybe a warehouse or storage unit.

The Mick was perched on a shelf across from the cot. It had crawled up the wall last night and stayed behind a box.

Now that it ventured away from its hiding place, Skizzy could see the object was a box of crackers.

"Well, I've heard of being in a dog house, mister." Skizzy set the remote in his lap and grabbed his coffee cup. He sat cross-legged on the chair, like a teenager playing Nintendo. This was actually how he would rather be spending his days. His mind was conjuring up other places to put Micks. Maybe the mayor's office or the IRS. Or maybe it was time to visit the White House, wear a floral shirt and hang a camera around his neck like any other tourist, leave a few Micks lying around. He would place four in the Oval office alone.

Chuckling at the thought, Skizzy started rocking, left to right, a slow rock while his fingers toyed with the remote. His body was swaying to some tune only Skizzy could hear. It was the tune from the movie *2001: A Space Odyssey*.

His eyes drifted to his surroundings. His makeshift bunker at least had food, water, lights, and computers. And it was larger, much larger than this hideaway the thief had chosen. And Skizzy's had bathroom facilities, although designed more for a bomb shelter.

"What the hell do you do for entertainment, dude?" Skizzy studied the screen, the images glowing amber, until the Mick bumped into something. It looked like a glass container of some sort. Skizzy put the Mick in reverse and brought the container into focus.

"What the..." He leaned closer to the screen and then jerked back. Inside the glass was a human finger.

* * *

"Of course he would keep the finger in some preservative," Dagger laughed. He adjusted the brightness on the monitor and studied the image the Mick was seeing. "Now if only you can get Mick to crawl outside and give us an address, you might be worth something, Skizzy."

"I can tell you now, I think that hatch thingy on the wall is a chute of some sort. Seeing that the walls are those old time cinderblocks..."

"Those are coming into vogue again. Sara's house is cinderblock."

"Hers was originally an auto dealership. This dude's building is old. Could be an old warehouse and deliveries were made through the chute, or a hospital or nursing home and it was a laundry chute."

"Or a coal chute. Some older homes had coal bins. Why don't you check that out, Skizzy."

"Sure. Like I got nothing else to do," Skizzy mumbled.

"You don't." Dagger clicked the END button on the telephone icon and smiled. He knew if it wasn't for his involving Skizzy in side jobs, the little guy would go crazy, or crazier in Skizzy's case.

"AWK, BAD BOYS BAD BOYS." Einstein lighted on the perch and ruffled his feathers.

"Who's bad, Einstein?" He reached up and stroked the macaw's bill. "Were you watching *Cops* again last night?" Dagger stood and clasped his hands gently around Einstein's head, examined his eye coloring. "You still look doped up, you know it?"

"DOPEY DOPEY, AWRRKK."

"It's a wonder you aren't falling off the damn perch." He watched as the macaw flew up to the catwalk and wrapped its claws around the railing. The macaw continued its screeching and drowned out Simon's appearance at the kitchen door. Several minutes later, the jovial postman was standing at Dagger's desk.

"Good aromas in that kitchen." Simon chuckled.

"I think Sara's making banana nut bread."

"Oh..." Simon paused, his smile fading, "Sara's baking?" Simon turned toward the couch, a chuckle catching in his throat.

Dagger avoided Simon's bait. He knew all too well how the scent of Sara's shampoo, bath soap, or a new body lotion, filled the room whether she was in it or not. It wasn't overpowering. You just knew she had been in the room.

"Pity about that professor," Simon said, turning serious and lowering his hefty body onto the couch. "Sara seemed to like him and she's a pretty good judge of character. You, on the other hand, are suspicious of anyone who looks sideways at that lovely thing."

"Including you." Dagger grabbed the rolled up copies of city maps he had obtained from the Building Department and carried them over to the couch. He no longer needed the isolated structure in the forest preserve for Sherlock's imaginary beast. But the maps might come in handy for his other case. After removing the centerpiece from the coffee table, Dagger opened the maps. "Where would you say the oldest homes in Cedar Point are?"

"Putting me to work, huh?" Simon leaned forward and studied the street maps. "Can I mark on it?"

"Help yourself."

Simon pulled a felt tip pen from his pocket and circled an area. "The First Ward is the oldest section in Cedar Point. Got a bunch of row houses along the state line." His pen circled another area in the middle of town. "Here is where the old city hall was and a lot of the surrounding houses are ancient." He eyed Dagger curiously. "Whatcha lookin' for?"

"Any houses that had utilized coal chutes."

"That would be most of them. Although near the old city hall, a lot of those houses were renovated. People dug out those coal rooms, practically chopping them off the building and adding on those fancy enclosures." Simon jerked a thumb toward the Florida room. "Sorta like that. Some put hot tubs in. Guess the mayor's project with them Philadelphia-style townhouses forced the residences to spiffy up their own."

"Our Evidence Room thief is living in an older house, one that has what looks like an old coal bin." Dagger slipped the top map off the table and watched as Simon studied the next map.

"Nope, this here's all new construction."

A bright splash of color swooped down from the catwalk and landed on the perch behind the couch.

Einstein let out a diatribe of screeches and squawks. Simon winced but it didn't phase Dagger. The detective was like a father used to the screamings of a house full of kids, immune to the sounds around him.

Sara appeared in the doorway to the aviary holding up a

braid of interlocking blocks. Brazil nuts were wedged between the knotted rope and Sara dangled the braid until she caught Einstein's attention. She carried it into the aviary and hooked it onto one of the tree branches.

The curious macaw flew onto the tree branch and hung upside down.

"Play time, buddy. That should keep you quiet for a while."

She closed the doors to the aviary and returned to the kitchen.

"Certainly takes care of her men, don't she?" Simon winked at Dagger.

"This is the last map," Dagger pointed out.

"Yeah, yeah." Simon studied the streets, reared back as if to get his bearings. "Nothing too old there unless you want to count the farmhouses in the unincorporated areas."

Farmhouses. Dagger wondered where he had heard reference to those before.

Simon unfolded his body from the couch and hobbled toward the kitchen. "Gotta see if that bread is cool enough to cut." He turned back and set something on top of the filing cabinet.

Dagger rolled the maps up and walked over to the desk. "What is it?" He eyed the three-inch-tall hourglass.

Simon grinned and elbowed his friend. "It's an egg timer." He was still chuckling as he lumbered off to the kitchen.

27

October 12, 1:45 p.m.

"You look like hell." Padre studied Marty's pallid face as the Indianapolis cop lowered his tired body onto a chair.

"Could use a little more sleep, like about a week." He looked around the chaotic office. "Any coffee and can they keep the noise down?"

The poor man was suffering more from guilt than a hangover, Padre determined. He set the cup in front of the cop and watched him lift the shaking cup to his mouth. "You may not remember, but when you were drunk you offered to escort Sherlock's body back to Indianapolis. Now that you are somewhat sober..."

"Yeah, yeah." Marty took a swallow of the hot liquid and winced. "When will the body be ready?"

"Can't release it til tomorrow, maybe."

"Maybe?"

"They are backed up in the M.E.'s office."

Marty seemed to digest the information, nodded grimly.

"Your guy made it easy for you." Spagnola's dark eyes danced as he stood in front of Padre's desk.

Padre glared at the smug detective with the gold pinkie ring and thick gold link bracelet. "Well, as you know, when you sit at the right hand of God, things just go your way." He forced a smile in return. Several years ago he had been partnered with Spagnola briefly but Padre learned quickly there were things Spagnola did that went against all rules. Like stealing money off dead bodies, jewelry from victim's homes. And once he had witnessed Spagnola planting a gun on a suspect. That had been the final straw. He told his partner under no uncertain terms would he keep quiet after the third such incident. Spagnola immediately asked for a new partner citing irreconcilable differences. That was fine with Padre. He didn't think Spagnola changed his ways, though. Just became more discreet.

"I kind of like the easy ones, too. My suspect hasn't committed suicide, but the case against him is unshakable." Spagnola left Padre with that little tidbit of information before strolling back to his desk.

"What was that all about?" Marty slouched in the chair, elbow on the desk, fist propping up his aching head.

"He thinks he has a pat case against Dagger. But you and I were with him the night Sheila's employee was murdered. Spagnola is spitting in the wind."

There were times Padre wished Dagger were a cop. He always thought he'd make a good one. He studied Marty's face, the crease above the bridge of his nose that seemed to have deepened since yesterday afternoon, the weariness in his eyes. All signs of burn out. Padre said, "You ever trust someone so much that it didn't matter to you that you didn't know everything about him? You respect him for who he is, no questions asked? And he trusts you, too, not to pry, to respect his privacy, and being a cop, that's hard to do, to not want to delve into his background. Ever know anyone like that?"

Marty's heavy lids blinked, and he nodded slowly, as if the sheer effort were painful. "Yeah,". he replied. "I'm escorting him home tomorrow."

"How is she doing?" Brian paced at the foot of Josie's bed as the visiting nurse checked his wife's blood pressure.

"As well as can be expected." She shushed him and pressed the stethoscope to Josie's chest.

He tried to keep his mind on his wife but he also had to find a buyer for the guns downstairs. Last thing he needed was to have them discovered in his house. Maybe it was best that they move away. Things were getting a little too hot. A change of scenery might do Josie some good, too.

The nurse straightened, stuffed her stethoscope and other implements into her black bag. She was gangly, arms and legs too long for her short midriff. Her thin face and short, black hair reminded Brian of Popeye's girlfriend.

"How's her appetite?"

"Next to nothing," Brian reported.

"It won't be long now," she whispered.

Brian walked her to the door and then returned to the bedroom. Laying the suitcase down, he opened it and checked the contents.

"What are you doing?" Josie's weak voice asked.

"Making sure you have everything you'll need." He moved clothes to one side and unzipped the storage compartment. Then Brian went downstairs and returned several minutes later with a bag of money. He stuffed the banded bills into the compartment with the rest of them. After snapping the locks on the suitcase, he set it on end next to the dresser.

"What about you?"

Brian smiled and sat on the edge of the bed. He thought back to the cache of weapons downstairs and the thrill of being on the road again, creating a new identity. He kissed Josie's freckled nose and said, "I travel light."

Skizzy studied the listings on realtor web sites. He figured that was the best place as any since realtors had a way of adding a little flair to nostalgic features of a home. They could gussy up the description to make a blackened coal bin sound like the perfect place to put a children's playroom. And it wasn't as if he expected the home to be on the market now which was why he was delving into their past sales or rentals.

He kept one eye on the monitor where Mick was waiting like some sniper in the dark. Skizzy had set it on action-activated so it would beep if anyone entered Mick's field of vision.

"Dammit, Dagger. Why can't your suspect be a female and frequent a health club so I can at least see something interesting." He checked the monitor again not sure if he had set the activation even though he had just checked it.

"Needle in a haystack," he mumbled as the printer spit out pages of property descriptions. What he was looking for was floor plans. If he could find a house with a coal bin the size he estimated and a door on the same wall as Mick had revealed, then he should be able to narrow down the search.

The buzzer upstairs rang and Skizzy turned his head to check the video of the person outside the pawn shop. The man appeared well-dressed and was carrying a gym bag with a designer name stamped on the side.

Skizzy pressed the speaker button. "Speak your business," he growled.

"Have some items to pawn."

The man looked safe enough. Looked like a banker and Skizzy envisioned him to have a bag full of his wife's china, probably trying to pay off gambling debts.

"Hang on a sec." Skizzy climbed the stairs and closed the bookcase, checking twice to make sure it stayed closed. After unlocking the dead bolts, he jerked the front door open.

"Come in." He checked up and down the sidewalk before closing the door. "What have you got?"

The man looked about twenty-five to Skizzy, and rich. The sweater was cashmere and the shirt had a button-down collar Skizzy thinks people called French collars. Mentally, he changed his assessment of the customer from a banker to a stockbroker trying to cover his losses with his parents' collectibles. Skizzy's eyes bugged as the man pulled several weapons from the bag and set them on the counter.

"I know this is very unorthodox for me to be coming

here with these weapons. My father is a preacher. Last Sunday's service he asked parishioners to turn in their weapons."

Skizzy held the short barreled rifle. "C15m? This is a military weapon." He checked two others. "Taurus titanium? Where do you live? In the middle of a drug cartel?" Skizzy always told customers he didn't deal in guns. Truth was, he would buy them but never sold them. Instead, he was stockpiling them in case of Armageddon.

The young man smiled. "My father always wanted his church to be in the center of the most problem-riddled part of town. He figures it wasn't the gang bangers who turned in their weapons. It was family members."

Skizzy was amazed at the light weight of the Taurus. Gun manufacturers had just started using titanium in their products.

"What do you think? I haven't a clue what they are worth."

"Steal these from your pappy?" Skizzy's gaze jerked from the pistol sight to the preacher's son.

"I'm sure the Lord won't mind us making a little money for the church. The rest of the weapons my father will turn over to the police." He held Skizzy's gaze with as much sincerity as he could muster.

Skizzy didn't believe him for a minute. His gut was leaning toward the stockbroker who lost a bundle in tech stocks. Definitely not the son of a preacher man. Skizzy was surprised the floor where the guy was standing didn't ignite in fiery damnation.

"Give you a thousand for all of it."

"A thousand?" the man sputtered. "The C15m is worth a hell of a lot more than that alone."

"Thought you said you didn't know what they were worth," Skizzy said, grinning. They settled on eighteen hundred dollars and as Skizzy slammed the series of dead bolts on the door he mumbled, "stockbroker my ass."

28

October 12, 5:20 p.m.

"You're a hard man to track down." Sheila pushed her way into Joe Spagnola's townhouse.

"I do have a phone."

"Must have lost the number." Sheila's gaze traced the room's dimensions, eyed the gym equipment in the middle of the living room, then noticed the towel draped around Joe's shoulder and the sweat glistening on his body. "A little light on furniture." Other than a television screen hanging on the wall and a geometric area rug under the gym equipment, there wasn't any other furniture in the living room. The complex backed up to a park and through the patio window Sheila could see a pond.

Joe stripped out of his soaked tee shirt. "Are you here as a damsel in distress or a pesky reporter?"

Her eyes glazed over the cop's chest, a patch of dark hair, damp and matted spreading from his sternum. His biceps were the size of her thighs and she felt a flutter in the

215

pit of her stomach. What was it with dangerous men she found so irresistable? She turned quickly and glanced into a side room near the kitchen. It probably was supposed to be a dining room, Sheila guessed, but instead there was a train set up on an eight-by-ten foot table.

"You have got to be kidding. You don't strike me as a Lionel Train sort of guy." She peered closely at the mini-town complete with trees, park benches, mountains, and miniature buildings. When she reached out to touch the coal car, Joe grabbed her wrist.

"Didn't your father ever teach you not to play with a man's toys?"

Pulling her wrist from his grasp, she held his gaze. "Only those with moveable parts." If Joe Spagnola had been in her high school, she just knew he would have been at the top of her father's list of boys to avoid.

Slipping around him and out of the room, Sheila said, "Just wanted to know if you had anything new on Caroline's murder." She pulled out a notepad and pencil to make her visit look official. It was warm in the apartment and she slipped out of her angora cardigan, hooking it over the handlebar on the exercise bike. A camisole under her silk blouse was sheer and Sheila wasn't wearing a bra. Her breasts were full and perky, the best Daddy's money could buy.

"Have a few good leads." Joe pulled his gaze from her and plodded off to the kitchen. "Want something to drink?"

"Wine would be great, unless all you have is carrot juice." She couldn't help but notice he filled out his gym shorts rather nicely. Her first impression was that he just recently moved in since his townhouse was sparsely decorated, and the subdivision was a new construction. "How do you entertain company without furniture?"

He returned with a glass of white wine and handed it to her. With a shrug he said, "I'm not a sociable kinda guy." Tipping his head back he downed his sport drink in one long guzzle. "You're welcome to wait while I shower but I really don't have much else to tell you." He didn't wait for her response, just headed for the bathroom.

The sounds from the shower drifted down the hallway. Sheila slid open the patio door. Joe's townhouse was on the ground level. A brick fence surrounded the one-hundred-twenty-square-foot patio and off to one side was a hot tub, simmering and bubbling.

"This is for us, Dagger." Stepping back inside, Sheila slipped out of her shoes and stripped off her clothes, leaving them trailing on the floor. On the couch was her purse, partially open, the corner of a tape peeking out. She stepped out onto the patio, slid into the frothing water, and waited.

29

October 12, 8:40 p.m.

"Einstein, what's wrong?" Sara walked into the dimly lit aviary and stared at the macaw. She probably shouldn't have given him another dose of medicine because all it seemed to do was make him lethargic. And she was getting used to his screeching. It felt comforting and she imagined it was the same way wives felt when their husbands snored. At least it filled the silence and there was a comfort in knowing you weren't alone.

Einstein blinked slowly and poked at his feathers with his beak. He spread his wings, showing her his vibrant blue underwings and then settled back on the branch.

"How about a warm shower? Would you like that?" Sara walked over to the shower and tapped the basin. The macaw looked past her, toward the window where darkness beckoned, but not for long. A faint glow in the night sky was arcing its way through the trees.

Einstein flew over to Sara and clamped his claws on her

arm. This startled her. Einstein would only land on Dagger's arm, never hers. She ran her hand over the silky feathers and down his beak. "Someone feed you avocados when our backs were turned?" Although the vet had said all tests for toxicity came up negative, Sara was never sure what Einstein might have eaten when she had him outside for exercise. "I'm going to have to stop giving you that medicine. It's difficult to tell your true symptoms." He grabbed a beakful of her hair and pulled. "Don't." She didn't know what it was about her hair. But he probably would try to grab her jewelry, too, if she wore any. "No," she scolded again. He released his hold and Sara stroked his back, pulled him closer. "You're just feeling uneasy because Dagger had to go to the police station, that's all. Everything will be fine."

She walked into the living room and looked out onto the darkened yard, the moon rising in the distance. A shiver ran through her. "It's almost over with, Einstein," she whispered into the macaw's crown. "This Friday the thirteenth rumor is just that, a rumor. I'll sleep down here tonight, okay?" She pressed her head against his and watched as the bright globe filled the sky. Even her grandmother had said if she stared long enough she could see the man in the moon. It was the craters or shadows that seemed to form the eyes and mouth. Even at a young age she hadn't believed there was a man in the moon. It was clear to her that it was only an illusion. But now as she stared she could see more than just the image of a face. She could swear parts of it were stained red.

* * *

9:25 p.m.

Dagger stood behind the chair, arms crossed, glaring at Detective Spagnola who was leaning against the two-way mirror. A tape recorder sat in the middle of the table, a tape in the chute. It was a stand-off. Spagnola wasn't going to sit until Dagger did, and vice versa.

"Where's Sergeant Martinez?"

"Ain't his case." Joe chewed his gum lazily and waited him out. As if being the good host, he asked, "How about some coffee?"

"No." Dagger didn't bother with 'no thanks' and watched Spagnola stroll out of the room. Dagger could just stroll right after him but he had no idea who was on the other side of the mirror. Finally, he pulled out a chair and sat down. He pushed the chair back, legs scraping against linoleum. The hard wood was uncomfortable as hell and he knew he wouldn't be sitting for long.

His gaze dropped to the recorder and it was obvious Spagnola wanted him to be curious, maybe even play it while he was gone. But he would wait him out. He wasn't that curious. Staring at the two-way mirror, Dagger slowly raised his middle finger and rubbed it along the side of his nose. Within a few seconds, Spagnola returned carrying a pad of paper and a cup of coffee that smelled several hours past brew time.

Detective Spagnola shoved the pad of paper at him, tossed a pen on the table and sat down. "Want to write out your confession now or after you hear the tape?" He smiled, a cocky smile like someone who felt he was holding all the cards.

Dagger smiled back. "Is it Tina Turner?"

"Close." Spagnola pushed the chute down and pressed PLAY.

The tape was a recording of his and Sheila's phone conversation earlier. But it had been altered. An expert job, too. On the tape Dagger was telling Sheila, "You can live here and take care of Einstein. Sara and I will be in prison." More editing and then Dagger's voice said, "It was a conspiracy. We planned it together."

Dagger silently seethed. Was Sheila in on it? Would she really go that far? "Did I ever tell you I have wonderful equipment that lets me know if my phone is being tapped?"

Spagnola's dark eyes danced and he leaned back, his chair touching the wall behind him. "Can't trust reporters, you know? They always want to get at the truth, no matter the cost."

"Did I also tell you, for business purposes, I tape my telephone calls and my tape definitely won't match this one?"

"Did you inform Miss Monroe her conversation was being tape?"

"Sure, right after she told me mine was being taped."

Spagnola nodded toward the pad of paper. "Just write down how you killed Caroline Kirby because you thought she was your fiancee."

"Ex-fiancee."

"So you admit it?"

Dagger smiled, folded his arms across his chest and turned his watch to see the time. "I have the best alibi in town. I was with one of Cedar Point's finest and one of the Indy P.D.'s finest. Just do your checking, unless that's too much work for you. Matter of fact, they can vouch for both me and Sara."

"Maybe you hired someone to do the job."

Spagnola leaned across the table, got up close. Dagger wasn't sure if he was trying to kiss him or what the hell he wanted. But he got a whiff of perfume and realized who it belonged to.

"You know," Spagnola whispered, "you shouldn't neglect your fiancee like that. She is one hot lady who needs it every day and night. Know what I mean?" He held his gaze, started that lazy chewing again.

Dagger realized Sheila was behind the tape, she was trying to get Spagnola to incriminate Sara. Sheila wasn't above doing whatever she had to do to get a story but to sleep with Spagnola to get him to doctor the tape was the final straw. Dagger knew the cop was looking for a reaction and Dagger wasn't going to give it to him.

"Don't worry," Dagger whispered back, "she's got her shots."

30

October 12, 10:05 p.m.

Skizzy leaned back in his chair and tossed a kernel of popcorn in the air. It hit his chin and landed on his chest so he picked it up and ate it. He tried another one, whiling away his time waiting for some action. This time, the popcorn hit its target. He checked the clock. It was past ten and nothing was happening. Not one to get to bed before midnight, Skizzy normally started his round of checking and rechecking the dead bolt locks about now. That usually took him two hours. During commercials when watching the news, he would recheck them. Then after he climbed into bed, he would be up at least ten more times making last-minute checks.

He decided to give Mick ten more minutes. Skizzy no sooner adjusted the contrast then the door to the room opened and a figure appeared on the screen. "Show time." He grabbed a fistful of popcorn. "Well, well, lookie here." Skizzy recognized the face on the screen. It was the same man who had shown up at the pawn shop claiming to have weapons collected by his preacher father. And he had a similar build and coloring as the man on the tape from the Evidence Room. "Preacher's son you ain't. And I doubt John Sinclair is your real name either." That was the name the young man had written on the sales receipt.

Something else was different. The man was wheezing, bending over, out of the viewing area of Mick. Skizzy made sure the tape was running. He moved Mick closer to the edge. But it still couldn't get a good view of the man without putting Mick dangerously close to falling off the shelf. The man still hadn't turned the light on in the room but it wasn't necessary with the night vision. Another strange sound erupted from the speakers and Skizzy adjusted the volume. "Well, you're sure in one foul mood, buddy." Scrapings, like a nail on a blackboard, made Skizzy cover his ears. "What in dad gum tarnation are you doing? Filing the serial numbers off those guns, I bet."

The figure on the screen rose, as if energized by some unseen cosmic force. Something else was different. The man staggered to the hatch on the wall and yanked on the lock, slapping it away as if it were a nuisance fly. The man inhaled the air and Skizzy watched as the muscles under the man's shirt strained against the fabric. There was something about the way he had slapped at the lock that caught Skizzy's attention but it happened too quickly.

Moonlight streamed in from the opening and Skizzy watched as the man tilted his head and soaked in those rays. And he seemed to grow. Skizzy thought it was his imagination, but the man was getting taller, bulkier. The back of the shirt split open as if he were some *Incredible Hulk* bursting out of his clothes. And when the man raised his arms to rip off the unwanted clothing, Skizzy saw what had caught his attention before. The man's hands were more like claws, hairy with long nails.

Skizzy fumbled for the controls to zoom in, get a closer image from Mick. But as soon as he touched the mouse, the man jerked his head up, as if he had heard the noise, the soft whirring from Mick, the inaudible tap-tapping of Mick's metal legs. Popcorn dribbled out of Skizzy's mouth as he was fixed in horror at the image on the screen. The head had transformed into something more animal than human, the mouth jutting out, teeth long. The fair skin was now covered with a mat of dark hair. And the eyes. As the creature searched for the noise, it's yellow slitted eyes ringed in red seemed to glow. It fixed on the bookshelf and located the mechanical spider. As if it had a mind of it's own, Mick backed away. Skizzy wasn't even aware his hand was still on the controls. When the creature jerked forward, its face pressed close to the bookshelf, Skizzy jumped back sending the bowl of popcorn tumbling to the floor.

But he couldn't pull his gaze from the screen. Mesmerized, he watched the creature draw back, a demonic laugh emitting from its mouth. It seemed to know it was being watched and didn't care. And it seemed to be performing as it retreated, folding into itself, morphing again, its arms developing into wings, its large bulk reducing in size to some winged creature. It seemed to levitate in front of the opened hatch before flying out.

Skizzy blinked, not quite sure what he had just seen. His

hand shook as he wiped the butter from his chin. "Goddam government experiments." He fumbled for the phone and dialed Dagger at home but all he got was the answering machine. He left a cryptic message for Dagger to call him ASAP. Then he tried Dagger's beeper and waited in the darkness of his bunker, wanting to play back the videotape but not sure he wanted to watch again. The thought of calling Padre crossed his mind but what would the cops think? That he was loony. Next thing he knew he'd be carted off to the nut house.

10:45 p.m.

Sara stepped out of the shower and dried off. After slipping into a nightgown she unfastened her hair and sat down at the dressing table. Her eye caught sight of the clock on the nightstand. Where could Dagger be? Did they arrest him? Running a brush through her hair she thought of calling Padre but then wondered if it were too late. But if Dagger were being held overnight, wouldn't he have called? She set the brush down and picked up the phone.

"I hope I didn't wake you."

Padre assured her she hadn't. Matter of fact, Sergeant Flynn was staying overnight at his house. Sara explained that she hadn't heard from Dagger.

"Would they keep him overnight without letting him make a phone call?" Sara asked, her one knuckle finding its way to her mouth. She nibbled nervously as she walked over to the windows and looked up at the moon.

"Definitely not. But I wouldn't put it past Spagnola. Let me make a few calls and I'll get back to you."

Sara hung up and went downstairs to check on Einstein. The medicine should have had him sleeping like a baby but he was on the perch in front of the windows in the aviary. She walked into the kitchen to make a cup of tea and wait for Padre's call. She didn't notice the blinking light on the answering machine on Dagger's desk.

11:15 p.m.

"Oh boy, oh boy. What do I do now?" Skizzy had been pacing and mumbling to himself for the past half hour. Popcorn crunched under his shoes and his hands were clammy. He pulled at his hair, a tuft which had already been shortened by his nervousness, jutted out from the right side of his head like a cowlick. "What did Dagger say? Fire? Yeah. We need fire. What else?" He paused at his desk and rifled through pages of notes. "Concrete buildings, unincorporated areas. Farmhouses. Yeah yeah. Gotta find the house. Let Dagger know." He dialed Dagger's beeper number again and kept dialing. Maybe if the thing vibrated continuously, Dagger might pay attention.

"Play back the tape, play back the tape." He pressed several buttons and with one hand still gripping the phone, he replayed the tape. Since Mick hadn't been destroyed and had night vision and zooming capabilities, it was possible Skizzy could catch some hint of the area outside of this guy's house. He watched the transformation again. Man to beast, beast to some winged creature. He played it in slow motion, feeling as if he were watching some sci-fi movie. No one could do that. It just wasn't possible. But neither are UFOs and aliens yet people claim to see them. Skizzy grabbed his glass and sniffed it, thinking someone might have slipped some hallucinogenic into his water. Maybe it was the accumulation of pot in his system from his youth. What he really wanted was for Dagger to see this on his tape. That would at least convince Skizzy that it wasn't his head playing some trick.

11:30 p.m.

It waited up in the trees, its body reclining on a large tree limb, feeling the lunar energy. It had shifted back to the beast, to its more powerful and speedy form. All it concentrated on was destruction, feeling its strength and power growing by the minute.

The sound of laughter pierced the air. The beast was at least a mile from any activity but its acute hearing allowed him to pick up sights and sounds never possible in his human form. This is what he had been waiting for since 1998. He had had a taste of power and the thought of experiencing that same exhilaration was mind-boggling, almost orgasmic. He had felt a hint of the energy during normal full moons, but nothing like this. Nothing like the combination of a full moon and a Friday the thirteenth.

Thoughts of his human life were a distant memory, pushed aside, as non-existent as this form would be by tomorrow morning. Josie, a vague remembrance of a whiny, clinging bitch, but a necessary evil. She had given him some semblance of normalcy, at least to the outside world. And there was a reason he had to be with her, he just couldn't think now what that reason was. Brian Andrews. He should know that name. But the only one that sounded familiar was Paul Addison. The Addison lifeblood pulsed through his veins. Unstoppable and stronger with each generation.

He stood and stretched his body. Almost seven feet tall. He could be as small or large as he wanted. He could slither under a rock or tuck himself into a blemish in the tree. Just by thinking it, his form could change. Such power. But something nagged at him. What was it? What was he forgetting?

Laughter again drifted to the beast's ears. It jerked its head up. Blood rushed and hearts pounded. Excitement, he could feel it, he could smell it. The sounds of his victims. Standing upright like some hairy neanderthal, it took a step into nothingness, its body plummeting, like an uncaped crusader, testing its skills, quickly maneuvering around branches as it fell, then folding its legs inward and imagining a large wing span. Instantly it shifted to a falcon and sped toward the source of the sounds.

"Come on, Steve. It's only dinner with my parents." The young woman clung tightly to her boyfriend's hand. "They won't bite." She looked up at the star quarterback for Cedar Point High School and admired his rugged features. Sunbleached hair and dimples, like he just stepped out of an ad for a tanning lotion.

"I'm sure I'm busy Sunday. Besides, all your father's going to do is tell me what play I should have used at third and ten."

"Well, he was a former coach, you know. Besides you two have a lot in common when it comes to football." Chrissy checked her watch. It was getting close to midnight, close to curfew and the last thing she wanted was to be grounded before the Sweetest Day dance.

"I'll get you home in time." He opened the passenger side door for her, walked around and climbed in behind the wheel. With a push of a button, the convertible top to his Mustang folded down. "Are you going to be too cold?"

Chrissy shook her head and cuddled up next to him, gathering his letter jacket around her. Steve turned the key in the ignition and put the car in gear just as he heard a loud hissing noise.

"What's that?"

"What's what?"

"Shhhh." Steve turned the car off and listened. The sound of rushing air was distinct. "Damn." He pounded the steering wheel. Tossing his phone in her lap he said, "Better call your parents. I think I have a flat. Matter of fact, I don't have a spare so ask your Dad to come out here. At least he'll know we're not lying about the flat tire."

Steve opened the trunk and retrieved a flashlight. Shining it on the rear right tire, he saw a large gash and the rim resting on the pavement. "Sonofabitch. Looks like someone slashed it." He set the flashlight on the ground and dug around the trunk. He could hear Chrissy pleading with her father, using her best Daddy's-little-girl talk on her old man. Grabbing the tire iron, he turned and felt something sharp enter his body. But he didn't feel any pain. He was too horrified at the site in front of him. His body was on total meltdown, felt a warmth spreading down his inner thigh and felt the tire iron slipping from his grasp.

"Okay, Daddy. We'll wait right here for you." Chrissy heard the tire iron clang as she ended the phone call. "He's on his way," she announced as she turned around and knelt on the seat. All she could see was the opened hood of the trunk, the moon illuminating the copper-colored exterior. "Steve? What are you doing?"

The night air was crisp and she could smell the residual of burning leaves. The car was parked on a side street a block from Dot's Diner, a hamburger joint the gang frequented after hitting the movies. But parking was scarce and Steve had been forced to park down an uncurbed and unlit street leading into an industrial complex. It was a good thing the moon provided some light.

"Steve?" Chrissy climbed out of the car and peered around the trunk. "Steve?" The flashlight lay on the ground beside the deflated tire. Maybe he hit his head, Chrissy thought. But the only thing lying on the ground by the trunk was the tire iron.

Bushes by the side of the road rustled and Chrissy felt chilled. Gathering the jacket tighter, she picked up the flashlight and headed toward the bushes. Maybe Steve was taking a leak. But why didn't he answer?

"Steve?" She shined the light on the opposite side of the road but there was just vacant land with dark buildings set back from the road.

Bushes rustled again. "This isn't funny, Steve. Are you taking a piss?" If all he was doing was trying to get her into the woods for a quickie before her father came, he had better think again. "I'm not coming in there after you." She shined the light toward the noise, saw the fall-colored bushes buck and sway.

This wasn't really a woods. She knew it was just unincorporated area, not that it made it less frightening. She entertained the thought of just leaving him here and walking back to the restaurant. But the restaurant was closed.

"Chrissy...help."

"Steve?" The voice she heard was more a painful moan. Panic swept through her body and she wrestled with the sudden urge to run.

"Chrissy."

Her name seemed to echo through the darkness, coming from above and even behind her. And she thought she heard a laugh, a soft, crazed giggle.

"Damn you, Steve. Quit scaring me." She flipped back her long, dark hair and mustered the courage. With a strong grip on the flashlight, she trudged forward, dried twigs snapping under her canvas shoes. "You are going to get this flashlight smacked right against the side of your head."

"Chrissy, help me," a voice whispered again.

There was something eerie about the way it sounded. More ethereal, disembodied. And Chrissy felt a cold sweep through her body. But she and Steve were alone here, right? He was the one who had forced her to sit through three showings of Blair Witch Project last summer. Now her mind was playing tricks on her. She never did like scary movies.

She heard another rustling, like someone scurrying through the woods, and shined the flashlight at the source. But all she saw were bushes and tree limbs swaying.

"Damn you," she whispered. She cautiously moved forward, toward a path which led into the woods. The beam from the flashlight brought the woods to life but pockets of shadows looked sinister and a voice beckoned.

"Chrissy."

This time there was no mistaking the pain in the voice. Maybe Steve stepped in a trap. Were there animals in these woods?

"Steve? Honey?" Her steps quickened as she moved deeper into the woods, gnarled branches reaching out to her, slapping across her back. Then she saw him, propped against a tree, his back to her. She rushed over to him. "Are you hurt?"

His eyes stared vacantly and she heard him say, "Put it back." But she didn't see his lips move. "Put it back," he said again. It was Steve's voice but his lips were frozen in a grimace. It was difficult to tell if it was the glow from the flashlight that made his skin look white and pasty or if he really was in shock.

"Put what back?" she asked him. "Steve, what's wrong?"

Slowly, her gaze dropped to his lap and she suddenly realized his brown shirt was soaked, pulled out of his pants, the bottom buttons missing. She wasn't quite sure she was seeing things clearly. A buzzing echoed in her ears, and her body felt lightweight, detached. Spots danced in front of her eyes and bile crept up her throat.

Steve's hands were in his lap, cradling his heart.

"Put it back," a disembodied voice said again.

Her arms and legs felt heavy, as though she were treading water. She vaguely remembered dropping the flashlight and trying to back-peddle away from Steve, away from the horrible scene in front of her. Try to get away, run. Her head was telling her what to do but she couldn't get her feet to cooperate.

Finally, she stood on shaky legs, and the most she could conjure from her vocal chords was a painful whimper and the word, "no" mumbled over and over again, until she finally found her voice, emitting a howling scream, and turning to stumble down the path. But it was blocked. She was frozen in mid-step, staring at a horrific-looking creature standing on its hind legs, its body covered in thick hair. But there was something cunning and human about it. It raised a large hand to its face, fist clenched with just one finger in front of its mouth. She could see a long purple talon jutting out from the tips of each finger, razor sharp and bloody.

Chrissy tried to scream but the sound was caught in her throat. This thing, this creature, smiled at her, and its large eyes glowed yellow. It shook its head back and forth slowly and said "shhhhhhhhhhhhh" from behind its finger.

31

Friday, October 13, 12:05 a.m.

"Spagnola is jerking his chain," Padre told Sara. "The desk sergeant told me Dagger hasn't been charged but if they don't release him within the half hour, I'm going to go down there."

"I hate to make you go out this late, Padre." Sara made another cup of tea and stood in front of the sink staring out at the large glowing ball in the sky. If everything was over with, why was she feeling this tremendous anxiety? Maybe Einstein was making her jittery. Maybe all this talk about Friday the thirteenth and a full moon and the professor's theory about shape-shifters had her panicked. Padre's voice sounded exhausted and she hated the fact that he had to spend all this time making phone calls but she knew how Dagger was about police stations. "Maybe I should go down there."

"You stay put. That's the last thing you need. According to the desk sergeant, Spagnola has a taped telephone

235

conversation between Dagger and Sheila where he admits both of you planned the murder."

"What!?" Sara set her cup down on the counter and marched to Dagger's desk. "That's ridiculous. I heard his conversation with Sheila. I can play back the tape for you."

"I believe you."

"Besides, why aren't they taking your word for it that you were with us that night? I don't understand why he is questioning Dagger at all." She noticed the message light blinking on Dagger's recorder.

"Politics, sweetheart." Padre sighed heavily.

"Dagger has a message. Hold on a sec." Sara pushed the PLAY button and heard Skizzy's frantic call for Dagger to check the recording from Mick.

"Sounds like Skizzy might have some movement from Mick," Sara reported. "Now all I have to do is figure out how to work this darn thing."

"Give me Skizzy's number. I'll find out what he's got. Doesn't look like I'm going to get any sleep tonight anyway."

"He won't talk to cops, Padre. Skizzy trusts us not to give out his number."

Padre mumbled, "Shit. Long as I'm up I may as well come over and see the damn tape for myself. And as long as the station is on my way, I'll stop by and end Spagnola's self-grandizing exhibition."

"I don't want to take you out of your way."

"No problem. It will do my heart good to get in that asshole's face."

* * *

12:17 a.m.

"This is fuckin' ridiculous." Dagger checked his watch. He had been cooped up in the interrogation room for hours. His beeper had been vibrating his body continuously and the only number on it was Skizzy's. "If you aren't charging me, I'm walking." He pushed away from the table and stood.

"I wouldn't do that." Spagnola rose and moved toward the door. Sweat stains ringed the underarms of his silk shirt and his unsmiling eyes challenged Dagger.

Ignoring the threat, Dagger walked to the door, hand on the knob. He wanted a reason to give this guy a few more facial scars. He heard movement in the room behind the two-way mirror and wondered how many armed officers were going to be in front of the door when he opened it. Instead, Dagger turned the lock and looked at Spagnola. It took the cop by surprise. He hadn't expected that. And Spagnola wasn't armed so Dagger needn't worry about getting shot.

Spagnola threw the first punch and hit air. He may have a few more pounds of muscle than Dagger, but he doubted he was familiar with the self-defense course Dagger had taken. Spagnola's face took on the frenzied look of a wrestler, the face of a growling linesman across the five-yard line. And when he let loose with a second punch, Dagger just grabbed the fist in mid-flight and with a jerk, flipped Spagnola through the air, his body landing with a thud.

"What's the matter? Swallow your gum?" Dagger taunted. He was vaguely aware of the scraping on the opposite side of the door, cops probably trying to maneuver a key in the lock. Spagnola jumped to his feet and Dagger's eyes never left his. Dagger raised his arms, slowly pulling his hair behind his ears. Spagnola charged but wasn't expecting Dagger's elbows to be just as dangerous.

Dagger barely moved, making Spagnola come to him. It was like playing racquetball. The smart player stayed in one spot. The inexperienced player was the one darting left and right, tiring himself out. Dagger's deep, inset eyes seem to recess even more, his elbows making tight circles, Spagnola making a major blunder. He was watching the elbows. And when the cop charged again, Dagger straightened his arm, the palm of his hand striking the cop on the forehead, then he made a wide arc with his leg and swept Spagnola's legs out from under him.

That was when the door burst open and four uniformed cops were on Dagger, pinning him face down on top of the table. He smiled at their efforts. It had taken them close to four minutes to get the door open. Now, like some wet seal, he slipped right out from under their grasp before the four youthful cops realized what was happening. Dagger stood watching them, smiling. Embarrassed, all four of them pulled their weapons.

Spagnola parted through the crowd and got into Dagger's face. "You just made one big ass mistake."

Dagger's smile broadened. Then he heard the clicking of the handcuffs and before he knew it Spagnola had him cuffed to that torturous hardwood chair.

Spagnola ushered the cops out of the room and wiped the blood from his mouth with the back of his hand. "I'll get your cell ready."

"I still get that one phone call," Dagger yelled at the cop's back. But Spagnola just closed the door.

The beast crouched on a large boulder like some grotesque gargoyle, studying the body of the young woman. There was something about her, something his human self had seen or heard. Something important.

It jumped from the boulder and landed next to Chrissy. Her eyes were lifeless orbs, her mouth frozen in a scream. Dragging a talon through her long brown hair, he felt a sudden surge, a brief tugging at his memory. It was the hair. Who else had long brown hair? Who else...? Then it hit him.

12:32 a.m.

Sara knew there was something in the communications program that would let her play back the recording of Mick. But without Dagger to show her what to do, she was afraid she might push the wrong buttons and erase the tape.

Checking the clock on the desk, she wondered again about Dagger. Why hadn't he called? And why wasn't Padre here? Sitting around doing nothing was driving her crazy. Sara ran upstairs and changed clothes. She looked like a ragamuffin in a denim dress. Shoving her arms into a denim jacket, she raced down the stairs, retrieved the keys to the truck and ran out the door.

The truck rattled down the drive. The remote control gate opened and the truck sped through. Maybe Dagger needed bail money. He had more than enough of it in his vault. She was just entertaining the thought of turning around to go back for money when she heard it.

Saraaaaaaaaaaaaa.

The truck swerved onto the shoulder of the road and skidded to a stop. Her heart pounded in her chest and she felt a cold sweat envelope her. How could it be? Wasn't the professor dead? Panic set in and she hugged the steering wheel. Peering through the windshield of the truck, she saw the massive ball of glowing light suspended over the road. The man in the moon appeared to mock her, its mouth in a hideous scowl.

What should she do? Where was it? Was it nearby? Is that why she hadn't heard from Dagger? Was he in the police station or was he dead? Had Dagger already lured it to the isolated building in Beacon Preserve?

Saraaaaaaaaaa, the voice called out again. *I know you can hear me.*

Sara put the truck in gear, made a U-turn, and sped down the road toward the preserve. The map Dagger had brought home showed a gravel road leading to the building. But it was too long of a drive. She had studied the map and noticed an unused access road near Fox Creek. The road could be grown over with weeds by now but at least it would place her closer to the building. The hawk would be able to see any activity taking place. Also, when she shifted, Dagger would be able to hear their conversation and know that the killer was still alive.

The handcuffs were starting to cut at Dagger's wrists. This wasn't fun any more. He should be home in bed, not placating a crooked cop. Thoughts of suing the hell out of the police department was the only thing amusing him right now.

He checked his watch and swore under his breath as he stared at the large face, the new toy Skizzy had given him. He had a telephone at his beck and call all along. Dagger pushed AUTO 1 and let the phone automatically dial Skizzy. Feigning exhaustion, Dagger pressed his forehead to the table, trying to get his mouth as close to the wrist phone as possible.

"What's up?" Dagger whispered. "I'm a little tied up right now."

"Dagger! Finally," Skizzy said, his voice in a frenzy.

Pretty clever of you, making everyone think the professor committed suicide.

Sara's voice echoed in Dagger's head. Clear and loud as if she were standing right next to him. An icy chill gripped him as he realized she wasn't talking to him.

I'm not just another pretty face. The beast cackled, a demonic laugh that sent a shiver up Dagger's spine. Between the blood rushing to his head and Sara's conversation in his head with the killer, Dagger could barely make out Skizzy's frantic explanation about the Evidence Room thief and how he was some kind of government creation that could fly.

What do you want? Sara asked.

Dagger wasn't sure whether to jump into the conversation or not. Did the beast know Dagger could hear them? Had to if he had heard them communicating during the warehouse bust.

Youuuuuuuuu, the beast replied.

"NOOOO!" Dagger screamed and jerked up, the cuff cutting into his wrist. *Sara, don't listen to him.*

Ahhhh, the knight wants to come to your rescue. But I think not. You'll be locked up tonight, Mr. Dagger. Can't help Sara this time.

SARA, DON'T LISTEN TO HIM, Dagger screamed in his head. He lifted the chair, hurling it against the wall, splintering it until the cuff was free from the chair. *If you harm one hair on her head, I'll kill you, you sonofabitch.*

Lesser men have tried. The beast laughed again, a piercing howl.

Now Dagger didn't care how many cops came in to subdue him and it seemed half the department was pouring in. He flung bodies over the table, against the wall, through the two-way mirror. A human wrecking machine completely oblivious of drawn guns and orders to get down on the floor. Somewhere in the commotion he heard Padre's voice.

"BACK AWAY, NOW." Padre shoved his way into the room while three officers held Dagger.

"He's still out there, Padre. Sherlock wasn't the one. He's still out there." Dagger nodded toward his wrist, his hair damp and clinging, eyes like a madman. "Talk to Skizzy."

Dagger blocked out Spagnola and the others, tried to concentrate on Sara and who, what, she was talking to, what they were talking about. At some point Padre had unlocked the cuff from his wrist and even unstrapped his watch.

"We have to go, now." Dagger pushed his way out of the room and no one tried to stop him. Spagnola was yelling something about having Padre's badge.

"Just give me his phone number. I can't talk on this damn Cracker Jack toy watch." Padre shoved the watch at Dagger. "And stop by my house. We have to pick up Marty."

Once they were in the Lincoln Navigator, Dagger punched Skizzy's number on the keypad and then pressed a button on the dashboard. The screen lit up and the red blinking light showed him Sara's location.

"We have a tracking device on the killer," Dagger lied.

Skizzy answered the phone on the first ring. "Why'd you hang up on me? What the hell's going on?"

Dagger told him to repeat everything so Padre could hear.

Skizzy spoke in a rapid clip, as though Dagger had given him a time limit. He explained what he witnessed from the surveillance at the home of the Evidence Room thief.

Dagger tried to concentrate on Skizzy but had to listen to Sara, too. She would be their only lead to the creature's location. But he didn't like what the creature was saying.

Ahhh, the police must have silenced your knight. I would have rather enjoyed destroying him. Now with him out of the way, it's just you and me. We can be so strong together, Saraaaaa.

* * *

The hawk didn't detect any movements when it located the isolated structure so it rose, carried high on the wind currents, and glided over the preserve searching for the beast. It heard commotion off in the distance and turned south to get a closer look.

"Put it up on the screen, Skizzy," Dagger said. Another monitor on the dashboard came to life and Skizzy started to play back the tape from Mick's surveillance.

I'm strong already. You can only shift during certain times. When was the last? March of ninety-eight? I can shift any time I want. Sara laughed at him.

Dagger's mind raced. What was she doing? Goading him?

"Holy shit," Padre whispered as the face on the screen changed, shifting into a hellish looking creature. "How the hell do we kill it?"

"Stick to the original plan, Skizzy," Dagger said as he maneuvered the Navigator around a turn and sped toward Padre's house.

Padre sank back against the seat. "That sonofabitch killed Sherlock."

"And probably Caroline Kirby too," Dagger said.

32

Friday, October 13, 1:30 a.m.

The hawk glided two hundred feet above the treetops. Not only could the raptor see in color but it also had ultraviolet detection capabilities. Its retina had two fovea for higher density versus the one fovea contained in a human retina. And although raptors had poor olfactory capabilities, this gray hawk's sense of smell was enhanced by Sara's shifting abilities, drawing sometimes on the senses of the gray wolf.

From its height the hawk had a good view of the marsh and woods where the creature might be hiding. Sara wasn't sure yet if by communicating with the creature it would be able to detect her location. But she couldn't stay silent forever.

What's the matter? Did I scare you away, Paul? That is your name, isn't it? Sara asked.

The beast ambled from limb to limb, distancing itself from the flashing strobe lights. The police had just arrived to check out the disabled Mustang. He smiled at the fren-

245

zied antics of the worried parents. Too bad he couldn't wait for the main attraction—the discovery of the bodies.

You are pretty bright, Sara. What else do you know about me?

Sara wasn't sure how far his powers extended. All she could hope for was by keeping Paul talking, Dagger might be able to pick up some hint of what the beast had in mind.

So Sara told the beast what the professor had found out about the Addison heritage. All the while the hawk searched for movement, searched for the beast which was difficult because it didn't know what shape it was in. What was becoming apparent as the hawk circled was that there wasn't anything else moving. It was as if every creature in the animal kingdom were in hiding.

"This is where we have to lure it." Dagger pointed to an area on the map. They were clustered around the coffee table in his living room. His hair felt damp and the shirt clung to his body. Although they had lined the handguns and clips on the couch, they all knew it would take more than a bullet to stop this thing.

Marty rubbed the sleep from his eyes. "Sure could use the professor about now. Where do we get the fire power?"

Dagger replied, "Skizzy is bringing that."

"Skizzy?"

"Don't ask. The guy is a cop's nightmare," Padre responded. "I could fill a citation book every time we cross paths."

"If he's got what it takes to kill this thing, I'll leave my citation book at home," Marty said.

"Skizzy will meet us at the mouth to the gravel road."

Padre looked up from the map. "I thought Skizzy doesn't own a car?"

"Not that the DMV knows about."

Padre tossed a look toward Marty. "See what I mean?"

Dagger found it difficult to concentrate and even harder to not join in on Sara's conversations. He didn't understand Addison's interest in her. Why waste time talking when he could be out killing? What was he hoping to accomplish? Had he never dealt with another shape-shifter? But what about his family?

Turning to Marty, Dagger asked, "How do we know there's only one? How do we know this Addison guy doesn't have a twin or some other male relative running around some other part of the world?"

Marty sank back against the couch cushions. Weary lines criss-crossed his face. He thought back to his many conversations with Professor Sherlock, trying to remember his exact words. "From what I recall from the professor's investigation, there can be only one."

"Only one?" Padre repeated.

"Yeah. Whenever a male was born on that certain day or came of age, whatever that means, he took over. The other dominant male in the family relinquished his power, energy. Usually relinquished meant died. If there were two, each would be half as powerful. But if there were only one..."

Marty's words faded as Dagger realized what the beast was up to. No wonder Addison was so fascinated with Sara's abilities. There can be only one. And right now there were two. How much more powerful Addison would be if he had Sara's abilities, to shift whenever he wanted, to not have to wait for a full moon on a Friday the thirteenth.

Dagger bolted from the couch. "When did Sherlock say was the exact time of the full moon? Three fifty-four?"

Marty shifted through Sherlock's notes, scanning dates and times. "Right." He hesitated, flipped back to the first page. "NO, that's Eastern Time. You're on central here, right?"

Dagger checked the clock. "Shit, that means it happens at two-fifty-four!"

2:25 a.m.

The vehicle lumbering up the road looked like a large shed on wheels. The men shielded their eyes from the glare of the headlights and the engine groaned to a stop.

"Holy shit," Padre whispered as Skizzy stepped from the Humvee.

He was dressed in a camouflage jumpsuit, military boots, with black paint on his face, and carrying a large contraption over his right shoulder. A chin mike was strapped to his head and an eye piece was flipped up.

"What the hell?" Marty whispered.

Dagger inspected Skizzy's equipment as if it were a piece of artillery he sees every day.

"Yeah, what the hell is it?" Padre studied the strange-looking weapon.

"M4 Module System machine gun. Known as a Land

Warrior," Skizzy replied in a monotone voice. "Currently in prototype stage and being tested in an underground lab in D.C." He held his toy up for the men to see, opening compartments, pointing to switches. "Has a range finder, day light video camera, video viewfinder, infrared and thermal sighting, a computer mouse control button relaying what I see back to Dagger's monitor."

Marty pursed his lips and shook his head. "Don't care how much fire power you have. It won't kill that thing."

Skizzy grinned. "Mine is modified." He pointed to his backpack. "I've got the biggest blow torch known to man. Like having a mini-napalm bomb on my back. Just point me at the sonofabitch."

While Skizzy showed his new toy to the cops, Dagger slipped into the Navigator to check on Sara. The red blip seemed to fan out in a circle. Right now Dagger had the advantage. The beast had set him up but he had killed Caroline rather than Sheila. Didn't matter to the beast. He accomplished what he wanted—got Dagger in jail and out of the way, or so the beast thought.

Why couldn't Sara have just stayed home? He and Skizzy could have handled it. How can he be expected to protect her when she was using herself as bait?

The red blip on the screen stopped, a steady pulse indicated the hawk was no longer flying. Had Sara found the beast? If so, how did she plan to lure it to Beacon Preserve? Up to now, Sara had been doing most of the communicating. Was the beast using it to his advantage, picking up her telepathic communication like a radar signal?

* * *

Don't you ever want to kill for the sheer thrill of killing?

No, Sara replied.

The hawk searched for movement, for life. Wind ruffled its coverts and parted the branches. It moved down several limbs, its gaze sweeping quickly. Turning, it dropped down another branch.

So naïve. I could really teach you a thing or two.

I doubt that.

The hawk felt the entire tree sway, as if something or someone was shaking it. It peered around the trunk to the opposite side. The beast was standing on the next branch. A shiver ran through the hawk. The beast was huge. It had a large protruding jaw and lips that curled over pointed teeth. Its hands and feet were scaly but there was still something human about it. Maybe the shape of the hands, its size, its cunning intellect.

Before it had seemed like a game of wits. Sara hadn't seen the beast. Can't fear what you can't see. Now that she had, she wanted to flee. The hawk was acting on instinct; Sara was on auto-pilot.

Cautiously, the hawk inched closer to the trunk and seeked refuge in a hollowed out section. It maneuvered its way inside and out of sight. The tree swayed again and as the hawk looked down toward the opening, it saw a scaly foot. Large talons scraped bark from the limb. The beast was on the branch right outside its hiding place.

Fear gripped the hawk as a horrible stench was carried in on the soft breeze. The beast smelled musty, like a closed up tomb. It smelled of death.

If anything were to happen it had to happen now.

You aren't very pretty, Sara said.

The sharp talons dug into the bark and the tree swayed again as the beast whipped around. The hawk could see the large taloned feet moving frantically in one place as the beast made a three-hundred-and-sixty-degree turn, realizing that Sara was close enough to see him.

"Jezzus, Sara." Dagger pounded the steering wheel. As long as he spoke the words out loud, he knew neither Sara nor the beast could hear. Sara had found Addison. She was letting him know that. He watched the red blip for movement.

Clever girl. Come out, come out, wherever you are.

The hawk felt the tree sway again, heard the rustling of tree limbs. Cautiously, it came out of its hiding place and observed the beast two trees away, standing behind the trunk, searching.

The hawk flew to one of the higher branches and gazed down. The beast had seen it. If it was as smart and cunning as Sara believed, the beast also knew that the only two animals moving tonight were it and the hawk.

They locked eyes, the beast sizing up the two-pound raptor.

Saraaaaaaaaaaaaaaaaa.

How high can you go? The hawk took to the air and climbed quickly. Glancing down, it saw the beast shift to a dark-colored bird, probably preferring a smaller bird for speed. Falcon's were known to kill other birds in mid-flight. The beast's wing-span was much wider than a normal falcon's. Unfortunately, it only proved to slow it down.

Sara knew there was just one way the wolf would kill. She had to lure the beast to the building she had seen on Dagger's map. Then she would have to do what she had told herself she would never do again. In order for the wolf to kill, the beast would have to witness her shifting.

Dagger pressed his forehead to the steering wheel. He watched the red blip move swiftly across the screen and he pressed a button to have the image zoom out. Sara was leading the beast to the target structure.

His black turtleneck was stifling and he felt the sweat trickling down his chest. The clock on the dashboard read 2:42 a.m. Through the windshield, he saw the full moon peering between the trees. Not much time left. He pulled his hair back in a rubberband, checked the clip on his Sig Sauer and jammed the gun in his holster. Bullets won't stop this thing but it just felt good knowing the gun was there.

Dagger exited the Navigator and walked over to the other three men. "He's nearby. We need to make our way to the structure but stay out of sight."

"How can you be sure he's headed there?" Padre asked.

Dagger hesitated. He couldn't tell them Sara was luring the beast there. "The professor said it goes into a killing frenzy at the moment the moon is at it's fullest, right? He should be able to detect us so we're setting ourselves up as its next victims." He checked his watch. "And we have about thirteen minutes left."

"Lucky thirteen," Skizzy mumbled.

They fanned out, weapons in hand, safety off. There was a damp chill to the air and a mist started to form. Dried twigs crackled under their feet and they stopped in unison to listen. The woods seemed void of any animal sounds. No owls, bats, birds, insects.

The three men stared at Skizzy, his eyes riveted on the Land Warrior, checking for movement.

The gray hawk dove from its altitude, reaching a speed close to one hundred miles per hour. It lighted on the limb of a tree just one hundred yards from the vacated building. The falcon was not far behind, landing just twenty feet from the hawk.

They sized each other up, eyes locked, unblinking. The hawk dropped to the ground and shifted into the gray wolf.

Impressive. The falcon dropped to the ground and changed into the beast, raising up to its full seven feet.

The gray wolf took a tentative step back. The beast smiled, it lips curled back, eyes rimmed in red, its talons poised and ready. Sara shifted to human and watched the beast hesitate, its gaze sweeping down the length of her body. But she had no plans for the beast to get more than just a peek. Quickly, she shifted back to the gray wolf and almost immediately the wolf bared its teeth, preparing to charge.

A maniacal laugh echoed through the woods. *This is the*

best you can do? A puppy? The beast reared back, its mouth wide in another hideous howl.

The gray wolf charged, catching the beast off-guard and tearing through its wrist with its sharp teeth, but causing little damage. It quickly discovered that the scales would be impossible to penetrate.

Bitch.

The wolf took off, heading in the direction of the building. It could feel the heavy footsteps of the beast, hear its raspy breathing.

If mist could be heard, it sounded like thunder. The four men exchanged looks as they felt the ground shake.

"What the hell is that?" Padre asked. He looked from Marty to Dagger. "Do you hear it?"

"Hear it, hell. I can feel it." Marty checked the clip on his gun.

Moonlight lit up the woods so visibility was good. But there were still dark pockets and the mist wasn't making it any easier, rising higher the deeper they penetrated.

"Got movement, got movement," Skizzy reported as he looked down at the screen on his M4. "Up ahead about one hundred and fifty yards."

They stayed close together. Crazy thoughts started running through Dagger's head. What if Sara gets mistaken for the beast? What if Skizzy or anyone of them starts firing before Sara can escape?

"Whoa, got two blips on the radar. There's two of 'um out there," Skizzy announced.

"Alive?" Padre asked. "Must have a victim." Instinctively, Padre and Marty gripped their guns tighter.

"Let's just not release a hail of bullets until we are sure what we're aiming at," Dagger said, fully aware Sara was close by.

33

Friday, October 13, 2:46 a.m.

There was only one way into and out of the building and the beast was quick to point that out. *And here I thought you were smart.* It stood in the opened doorway, getting its bearings, searching. It inhaled deeply, feeling the surge of power from the moonlight penetrating its back. Slowly, it entered. The beast swatted empty fifty-gallon drums aside as if they were made of paper. The floor was concrete and its talons scraped with each footstep. *Where's your knight in shining armor now?*

Sara was no longer in control. When there was a witness to her shifting, the wolf took over. It was as if she were watching a movie. Only a viewer, not a participant. She shuddered at the thought of watching the wolf kill, of feeling the life seeping from a being, no matter that the beast deserved it. Sara hoped Dagger arrived in time so the wolf wouldn't have to do the job.

What? Cat got your tongue? The talons tapped on the

concrete as it edged closer. Its eyes glowed and red appeared to seep from the corners.

The wolf knew it was out-sized and out-powered but it would fight to the death. And Sara knew it was close to that time, close to those three minutes when the moon was at its fullest.

The beast was pacing now, its fists clenching, its powerful forearms crashing into whatever stood between it and the wolf. It was in a frenzy because it needed Sara's power and it could only get it as long as the moon was still full. Once the moon started waning and Addison shifted back to his human form, it would no longer be able to absorb Sara's energy.

A voice from somewhere outside shouted, "IN HERE, IN HERE."

The beast was distracted momentarily, enough time for the wolf to charge at the beast's throat. But the beast's reflexes were lightning quick. With one quick swoop, it back-handed the wolf sending it crashing against the concrete wall where it crumbled to the ground and lay motionless.

The beast paused. It could still hear the wolf's heartbeat. It was still alive. The thirst for power and energy was all-consuming. Somehow it knew it had very little time left. It descended on the helpless animal.

Padre held the light up as they entered.

"Careful," Marty cautioned. "What is that?"

Padre swung the light around and it shone on the overturned barrels. The light was a high-intensity beam which created dark pockets behind the drums.

The building smelled damp and musty, the air stale. But there was a rotting odor too, as if animals had seeked shelter in the winter only to freeze to death. It was no longer used for anything, much less storage, and what little was in here looked as if it had been left to rust or mildew.

Dried leaves, swept in over the years, were wedged in the corners. There were only two windows, its panes fogged with grime and age, the locks rusted shut. A section was condoned off on the far wall. It resembled an empty stall, three-sided, about ten-feet deep and five-feet wide.

The four men stood in an arc in front of the doorway listening. Dagger hadn't heard much from Sara and all he could think was the worst. Perhaps they had left already.

"What do you show on the meter?" Dagger asked Skizzy.

"Still got two blips straight ahead."

They fanned out and Marty switched on a second light.

"Just up ahead," Skizzy shouted.

Both high beams were aimed at the far wall. There were two wolves lying ten feet from each other, identical in size and color.

Dagger remembered the papers from Professor Sherlock's briefcase. The beast could shift into any form it wanted. It was cunning enough to shift to a form identical to the gray wolf.

Sara? All Dagger could hope for was a response before Skizzy's trigger finger annihilated both of them.

"That don't look like what I saw on the screen," Padre

said.

"It can camouflage itself," Marty responded.

"Just kill 'um both." Skizzy raised his weapon.

"Wait." Dagger bent down and studied the two animals. He could see the chests on both rising and falling. They were both still alive. *Sara?* He tried again to communicate. Suddenly, eyelids fluttered on one of the wolves and it began inching toward Dagger. *Sara?* Dagger watched it approach just as the eyelids on the other wolf moved.

Dagger? It was a weak response but Dagger wasn't sure which animal it came from. "Shit." He wiped a forearm across his face.

"What are we waiting for?" Marty yelled. His weapon was grasped tightly, arcing from one wolf to the other.

The wolf closest to Dagger continued crawling. But something was wrong. The wolf lifted its eyes toward Dagger and whimpered, struggled to its feet. Dagger's gaze shifted from the wolf still lying prone several feet away to the one edging closer.

Sara? Dagger cautiously touched the wolf. It looked up at him and whimpered again. How could he be sure?

"We don't have much time." Marty yelled.

Dagger lifted the ninety-pound wolf as he cast a final glance at the wolf lying prone, its eyes fully open. He yelled, "NOW!" and heaved the wolf into the stall, its body slamming against the back wall.

It shifted momentarily to Paul Addison. Naked and startled, Addison attempted to shift back to the beast. But Skizzy's M4 spit out a stream of molten lava which clung to Addison's skin and engulfed him in a fiery blaze.

Skizzy yelped out a roaring battle cry. Out of instinct, the other three men unloaded their weapons and watched in horror as Addison tried to shift into the beast, briefly rising up to its full seven feet, a painful howl coming from its mouth. It tried shifting to its winged counterpart but the wings quickly caught on fire. Addison was like a toy transformer, mixing body parts, trying desperately to remain all beast so it could regenerate. But the fire had consumed its human side and that was the only way it could be destroyed.

The men stood for five minutes, like a small band of marauders not quite sure if they could claim victory. They were mouth-breathing, gulping in loud breaths, their eyes fixated on what had briefly resembled a rather attractive man, fair skin, slight build. If they hadn't seen Paul Addison in the flesh for themselves, they would have never believed what he had become.

What was left of Paul Addison had been incinerated to a pile of dust that could fit in a cigarette case. Nothing had moved, no body parts came to life, and the ashes hadn't reassembled like some *Terminator* cyborg.

"Is it over?" Marty whispered.

Instinctively, Dagger checked his watch. It was three o-clock. He suddenly realized the other gray wolf was gone. "SARA!" He grabbed one of the flashlights and rushed out of the building.

"DAGGER!" Padre called out after him.

Dagger followed a trail of blood through the woods. It headed in the opposite direction of the gravel road. He soon located his truck and the figure lying twenty feet away. The front of Sara's dress was soaked in blood. He tossed the flashlight down and dropped to his knees.

"Sara." He whispered her name as he gathered her in his arms. Lifting her dress, he saw the extent of her injuries and groaned. "My god, Sara." He was cradling her when Padre and Marty caught up.

"Jezzus. What the hell is Sara doing out here?" Padre asked.

"I forgot. She said she was going to meet us here."

"Have to get her to the hospital."

"Is she awake?"

"Take her pulse."

All the voices were swimming in his head and Dagger didn't think an ambulance could get there in time. His arms were shaking as he held her and he vaguely remembered Padre feeling for a pulse and telling him it was thready.

Dagger pulled the blue jean jacket tightly around Sara and lifted her. Her arms hung limp as he carried her to the truck. He didn't remember who drove but they arrived at the hospital in record time. He had always heard of people being numb after a catastrophe and now understood what it meant. Dagger was going through the motions, movements jerky, eyes not focusing, head bobbing as if on some moveable spring.

Sara was so pale he didn't think she had an ounce of blood left in her. Dagger didn't know how to pray, didn't believe anyone could listen to insignificant humans. So he found himself talking to Sara's grandmother. Ada would know what to do if she were alive.

* * *

The Emergency Room was bustling and it wasn't until Padre forced Dagger to sit down that he realized everyone in the waiting room was staring at him. Then he looked down at his hands. They were covered with Sara's blood. His clothes were, too, but didn't show against the black colors.

Padre mumbled something about Marty and Skizzy staying back to clean up the mess. Skizzy wanted to treat the ashes to one more blast of fire power. Dagger leaned forward, elbows on his knees, clasped hands pressed to his forehead.

His mind toyed with images of Sara. Her playing with Einstein, weeding the garden with her dress hiked up revealing her shapely legs, her laugh light and airy. And those eyes. It was the eyes he had seen on the wolf that was lying prone. Those turquoise eyes that told him which wolf was Sara. He also remembered both the gray hawk and gray wolf were timid around him. So the gray wolf that had eagerly approached him couldn't have been Sara. He pressed his fingers against his lids and sighed heavily.

Slowly, Dagger ran his hands through his sweat-soaked hair. At some point he had lost the rubberband and as he stared at his stained hands, he wondered how much blood was smeared on his face. He had done his best to press his body against Sara's to try to stop the bleeding.

"Mr. Dagger?" A soft-spoken nurse whose face reflected the worst looked down at him. "The doctor would like to talk to you."

Dagger stood on rubbery legs and told Padre to wait. He

followed the portly woman down a corridor and through the double-door that said "Emergency Room." The nurse led him past three curtained cubicles and pulled open the curtains to the fourth. Dagger braced himself, expecting the worst.

A bearded doctor with a perplexed look on his face was holding Sara's wrist and checking his watch. He waited several seconds, gently placed Sara's arm down, and stepped back.

"This is Doctor Reynolds," the nurse said.

"You brought her in?" the doctor asked.

"Yes."

"And you are?"

"Chase Dagger. We're business associates."

Reynolds picked up Sara's bloody dress and laid it across the foot of the bed. "As you will note, this dress isn't torn, cut, ripped, nothing."

Dagger checked the fabric. He was right. But that didn't surprise Dagger. Sara wasn't wearing the dress when she was sliced open by the beast.

Reynolds then lifted Sara's hospital gown, revealing her midriff down just to her hip bones. "And no injury."

Dagger blinked. He had checked her injuries and seen the claw marks when he held her in the woods. Three deep gouges ripping her open from sternum to below her waist. Sara's body had healed itself already. He felt a surge of relief and fumbled his way from the foot of the bed to Sara's side.

"Why isn't she awake?"

"She's in shock. Think she might also have a concussion. We'll do some X-rays, keep her overnight for observation."

Dagger clasped Sara's hand. The skin was pale but soft and he kissed the top of it.

"I don't suppose you know whose blood was on her?" Reynolds tilted his head back, eyes inquisitive, suspicious.

All the events of the past five days were details that would not see the light of day. Dagger stared at Sara's prone body. "There's a Sergeant Jerry Martinez in the waiting room if you want to find out details." Dagger didn't feel like talking and was sure Padre wasn't going to say much either other than they were apprehending a fugitive.

"Is it all right if I spend the night with her? She's never been in a hospital before and it might be best if I'm the first person she sees when she wakes up."

34

October 13, 1:25 p.m.

Dagger had tried to sleep during the night but it was impossible. The chair was uncomfortable and he was too worried that Sara might wake up and not know where she was. A number of times it seemed as if she were having nightmares, fending off some imaginary fiend, moaning and crying, and one time screaming, which sent the night nurse tearing down the hall.

After the nurse had left, Dagger lay next to Sara and held her. That was probably the only fifteen minutes of sleep he had gotten all night.

Padre had called to tell him they had located the farmhouse where Paul Addison lived as Brian Andrews. Skizzy's Mick had revealed a marker across the street from the house, a tag from the gas company, and a corn field. They were going through the house now and speaking to the neighbors.

Dagger scratched the stubble on his face and stared out

of the window to the parking lot four stories below. The sun was glaring. The world was unaware of what had transpired last night and it was best they were kept in the dark. Besides, no one would believe them.

A nurse came in with a tray, checked Sara's vitals and took a blood sample. Sara stirred and Dagger looked over to see her eyes blink slowly, trying to focus on her surroundings. What the nurse was doing registered immediately.

"About time you woke up. Still feeling groggy?" the nurse asked.

"NO!" Sara struggled to get up from the bed.

"It's okay. I'll handle it," Dagger told the young nurse who had been startled by Sara's sudden outburst.

"Sara, you're in a hospital." Dagger sat on the edge of the bed, his fingers brushing her hair from her face.

"No." Her gaze followed the nurse out of the room. She tried again to pull herself out of bed. "You promised," she cried. "No hospitals."

He held her close and she struggled against him, mumbling, "you promised." She wept into his shirt, her body trembling.

"I couldn't help you like your grandmother could. I had no choice, Sara." He held her close, making shhhing noises, her body weak and trembling.

She held onto both of his arms tightly as he pulled her away, forced her to look at him. "I had no choice. I couldn't let you bleed to death."

"You promised." Her sobbing was uncontrollable now and she fought him, grabbing handfuls of his shirt, but soon relented and let him hold her.

Dagger gently cupped her face and kissed her forehead, then her bruised cheek. Her eyes reflected her anguish, the color dull. He imagined it would be awhile until her ordeal was a slight memory and doubted any of them would ever fully forget.

"I trusted you," she said, pressing her head to his chest.

"Your grandmother trusted me to keep you safe. This was the safest place for you," Dagger whispered as he stroked her head. "They didn't hurt you."

He felt her head shake side to side under his chin. Her sobbing increased and he could barely make out what she was saying.

"You let them take my blood," she whispered. "They can't take my blood. They'll know it isn't normal."

"What?" Dagger grabbed her shoulders and gently pulled her away, stared into her tear-streaked face. "What do you mean?"

"They'll know, Dagger," she sobbed.

Finally the realization hit him. She had more than just human blood running through her veins. "Jezzus." He rushed out of the room and searched the halls for the nurse with the cart. He asked a young woman at the desk, "Where did the nurse go, the one taking the blood samples?"

"Probably to the lab on the second floor."

Dagger ran to the elevators but opted for the stairway and dashed down the two flights. Following the signs leading to the lab he wondered how he was going to get the sample if the cart had already been wheeled in. But he lucked out. The nurse had made another stop and he found the cart parked outside the door to one of the rooms.

Dagger scanned the names on the vials. They didn't seem to be in any particular order. The thought of just tipping the whole cart over with hopes all the vials would be destroyed crossed his mind. But that would be messy and there was no guarantee Sara's would be one of the ones broken.

He heard the nurse coming just as he located Sara's vial. Pulling the sample from the tray, he double-checked the name and headed to the closest restroom where he opened the vial and flushed the contents down the toilet. After rinsing the vial in the sink Dagger tossed it in the garbage can by the door. He was sure he must have violated some disposal law. Exiting the restroom, he was surprised to see Padre and Marty stepping off the elevator.

"Hey, we've been looking for you." Padre said. He steered Dagger onto the elevator.

Before Dagger could ask Padre what he told the Emergency Room doctor last night, Marty said in a rushed voice, "She's on seven."

"Whose on seven?" Dagger eyed the two men who nervously watched the floor numbers light up.

"We checked out the house where Paul Addison lived," Padre explained. "Found more weapons, Officer Riley's finger, and found out something interesting from the closest neighbor." The elevator dinged and the doors opened onto the seventh floor. "Addison had a wife."

Marty whipped out his notepad as the three men approached the nurse's station. Dagger looked around the floor and realized where they were.

"Yeah," Marty confirmed. "It's the Maternity Ward."

Every nerve-ending Dagger thought was numb from last night came alive. "Paul Addison had a wife?"

"Brian Andrews, same difference. Her name is Josie," Padre said. "According to the neighbors she was brought in some time last night."

"May I help you?" The name tag on the nurse with the short-cropped hair said *Linda*.

"Josie Andrews. We understand she was admitted last night." Padre held up his shield.

"Oh," Linda gasped. "Is there a problem?" She thumbed through a stack of folders on her desk. "Haven't had a chance to file them away." Josie's folder was near the top. "Here we go." She opened the file and took a quick glance. "Yes, she was admitted at one-fifteen in the morning." Glancing up at the men, she raised her eyebrows as if to say, "and you want to know because?"

"And?" Padre said, his hand circling as if winding her up.

"Oh," she perused the patient chart and smiled. "She had a nine-pound-two-ounce baby boy at two-fifty-four."

"Two-fifty-four?" Marty parroted.

"That's what the chart says."

The three men stared knowingly at each other, their minds reeling with Sherlock's words: The evil is passed on from generation to generation.

"I'd like to speak with Mrs. Andrews," Padre said.

"She isn't here." Linda looked past Padre at a figure approaching. "Doctor Foster," she called out. A stocky man in blue scrubs made an abrupt stop. "These gentlemen need to ask you about Josie Andrews."

Padre showed the doctor his shield and introduced the other two men. "Is there some place we can talk?"

The scent of antiseptic soap trailed behind Doctor Foster as he led them to a room at the end of the hall. It was a small waiting room with two couches and a dimly lit table lamp.

Doctor Foster explained how Josie had had a difficult pregnancy. She had been spotting the last four months so he had restricted her to complete bed rest. It hadn't helped that she had gained fifty pounds.

"Had you ever met her husband?"

"Just once. I stopped by their house to bring Josie a prescription. He seemed a nice enough fellow. Very attentive to his wife." He studied the faces of the three men. "What is this about?"

"Seems her husband isn't such a nice guy and we were hoping to ask Josie a few questions," Padre said. "Did you know she left the hospital?"

"That's what the nurse told me. It certainly wasn't with my approval. They took the baby in to her at nine this morning. When the nurse returned at ten o'clock, mother and child were gone."

Marty was quiet, staring at his notepad, folds of skin sagging under his eyes.

Dagger checked his watch for the third time, wanting to get back downstairs to Sara.

Marty asked, "Did she tell anyone where she might be going?"

"I would assume home."

Padre shook his head. "Place is cleaned out, at least of clothes so whatever she brought with her here is all she is taking with her."

"What about the baby?" Dagger asked, glancing at his watch again. "Any birth marks?"

"I would like a copy of his footprints," Padre said.

"Of course. The baby was fine. No noticeable birth marks." Foster paused and thought for a moment. "Although he did have a club foot. Not too unusual being cramped in close quarters like that for so long. But Josie was adamant about seeing a specialist." He reached under his scrubs and dug into his pants pockets. "I gave her the names of a few specialists. She didn't seem to care where they were in the country." He opened a notepad and handed it to Padre. His hands were as smooth as a baby's as he pointed to the short list, and the antiseptic odor wafted through the air again.

Someone's beeper went off and the doctor, Padre, and Marty, all checked to see if it was theirs. Dagger's beeper was set on vibrate so he knew it wasn't his.

"I'm sorry, I have to leave," the doctor announced.

Padre and Marty each handed him a business card and asked him to get in touch with them if he thought of anything else or if Josie or one of the specialists gets in touch with him.

The three men watched the doctor leave but remained in the waiting room. Dagger reached out and gave the door a shove. It closed with a soft click.

"Think Josie knows about her husband?" Dagger asked.

Marty shook his head. "According to the professor, the Addison wives were pretty much kept in the dark. He might have left her instructions to take the baby and run if one day he failed to show up."

After several more moments of silence, Padre asked Dagger, "How's Sara?"

"Still critical but she'll be okay. She was shaken up pretty badly."

"But what about her injuries?"

Dagger blinked wearily. There was so much he couldn't say. "It looked a lot worse than it was."

Marty closed his eyes as if in deep thought and all three men were startled when somewhere down the hallway a food tray clattered to the floor.

"Be a long time til things are back to normal," Padre said, a shiver pulsing through his body. He leaned back, a slow smile spreading across his face. "That Skizzy is something else. All he kept saying is 'goddam government experiment.'" Then he started to laugh, an hysterical giggle and he soon had Marty laughing along with him. Call it a sudden surge of relief that it was all over or reverse shock. "And that Land Warrior weapon of his weighed more than Skizzy." Padre was in an all out belly laugh now, tears streaming down his face. "It's a wonder the first blast from the damn thing didn't back kick Skizzy to Florida."

Dagger couldn't help but smile. It was over, at least for Paul Addison. And it was for Sara, too. But was she okay emotionally? Would she ever be the same or did this change her? She had been in the throes of it all. It would be hard for her to see the same humor in it that Padre did.

But at least Marty would probably retire now. Unfortunately, Sherlock didn't live to see his worst fears confirmed. The six-year-old boy who had witnessed the death of his parents and brother, hadn't imagined it all. It really had happened.

The laughter slowly subsided. Marty pressed his head against the wall and stared at the ceiling. After a few moments, he shifted his gaze to the two men and said, "In case anybody's interested, June 13, 2014 is the next full moon on a Friday the thirteenth."

35

"Mr. Dagger, I'm so glad I found you." Miss Collins, the second floor nurse hustled him down the hall as soon as the elevator doors opened on the second floor. "She's gone," she announced.

"Sara?" Dagger ran to Sara's room to find a hospital gown lying on the bed. "Are you sure? You've checked the halls? They didn't take her back down to X-ray?" Dagger checked the bathroom.

"We've checked every conceivable place. She must have stolen someone's clothes or hospital scrubs." Motioning to the stained denim dress, Miss Collins added, "And she obviously didn't wear her dress."

Dagger's gaze drifted to the opened window. Sara couldn't have shifted in her condition. She didn't have the strength. But if she did, there was one way he could locate her.

* * *

Dagger turned the key in the ignition and switched on the monitor on the dashboard. He breathed a sigh of relief as he saw the red light blinking, showing him Sara's location. According to his map, Sara was in the vicinity of her home.

Sara? He waited for her response. When he didn't get one, he could only assume she was home and had already shifted back.

He put the Navigator in gear and tore out of the parking lot. It was a twenty-minute ride home. If he pushed it, he could cut it to twelve minutes. Punching the auto dial on the console phone, he listened to the answering machine. Sara wasn't picking up the phone.

Why did she leave the hospital so soon? She was definitely in no condition. But she would heal quickly, she had already proven that.

Dagger raced the SUV down the driveway, not even bothering to pull the Navigator into the garage. According to the tracker, Sara was inside the house. He parked at the front door and ran inside. Hopefully she was in bed getting some rest.

There was no sign of Sara on the living room couch. The two doors to the aviary were shut firmly, the way he had left them yesterday. After poking his head into the kitchen, he quietly climbed the stairs to Sara's bedroom. It was empty.

Puzzled, he checked her bathroom. Still no sign of Sara. Standing in front of the balcony window, he searched the backyard. Maybe she felt the need to go to Ada's grave out back. *Sara?* No answer. "SARA," he called out. She had to be some place in the house, Dagger thought. Now she was starting to worry him.

Rubbing the back of his neck, his gaze dropped to Sara's dresser. Her stud earring, the one he used to track her, was lying next to the lamp.

"SARA!" Dagger ran out of her room and down the stairs. He alternated calling her name out loud and telepathically. First he checked the garage to see if any of the cars or the truck were missing. They were all there. Then he climbed into the Navigator and raced out to the back acres where her grandmother was laid to rest.

Sara, I got the vial back. I made it right. He waited for her to respond as the Navigator bumped its way through the acreage. *Sara don't do this. You're scaring the hell out of me.* He brought the Navigator to a stop and ran up to the gravesite, which overlooked a creek. Sara wasn't there. Exhausted and emotionally spent, Dagger dropped to the ground, kneeling on the damp grass. He apologized again to Sara explaining that it was a mistake. He didn't know about her blood and promised to never do it again. *DAMMIT SARA.*

Then he started apologizing to Ada for not taking care of her granddaughter, for putting her in jeopardy. *Just let her be all right*, he told Ada, as if he believed she could really hear.

Dagger spent the next four hours cruising the streets near the hospital, extending his search to wooded areas until darkness made it impossible. Then he went home for his night vision goggles and continued his search through the woods.

He succumbed to his curiosity and returned to the isolated structure where Skizzy had killed the beast, thinking Sara might have had the same macabre impulse—to make sure it was really dead.

The first difference he noticed was the night sounds. What had been an eerie silence last night was teeming with activity tonight. Cautiously he stepped into the building, his flood light illuminating the concrete floor, the trail of blood to the doorway. Finally, it settled on the alcove where he had thrown the beast. The floor and walls were charred. The beast had been reduced to soot.

Slowly he turned, the flood light spilling into the corners but there still wasn't any sign of Sara. He had tried communicating with her during his search. He had told her about Josie Andrews and the baby that had been born. How Padre and Marty were hoping to locate Josie and her baby by contacting the specialists. They just didn't know what they would do when they found her. He laughed when he told her that Skizzy was right. That the doctor will probably place a chip in the baby so they could monitor its whereabouts in fourteen years.

Exhausted, he returned home and sat on the catwalk in front of the windows, staring out at the yard. He could swear he saw Sara dancing, twirling, shifting into the gray hawk and then the gray wolf. But when he blinked the fatigue from his eyes, there was nothing in the yard but emptiness.

Padre offered to put out a missing person report on Sara but Dagger told him she was his responsibility. He would find her. Only problem was, he didn't know where else to look.

He spent the rest of the week in a drunken stupor. Even Simon couldn't console him, and to his credit, never made jokes or told him "I told you so." Dagger didn't return phone calls, especially Sheila's.

By the second week even the liquor didn't taste good. Einstein stopped talking and would join him on the catwalk just staring out into the yard, refusing his favorite cheese curls. Dagger never stopped trying to communicate with Sara, never stopped hoping she would respond.

During the third week when Dagger made one of his frequent trips to Ada's grave, he promised Ada he would do a better job next time. Just keep her safe. He could swear he heard Ada say, *She needs some time.*

At the end of the third week, Dagger finally shaved. He continued to sleep in Sara's room, hoping some night she might come home. The patio door was left open in case Sara returned while he was sleeping. He refused all cases that came his way and spent the days reading the newspapers and her favorite magazines to her.

By the fourth week, he trudged through the first dusting of snow to Ada's grave. The wind whipped his ankle-length trench coat around his legs and he brought one of the thick blankets Ada had woven. Wrapping the blanket around his shoulders, he huddled on the ground. He told Sara about the new toys Skizzy had invented and how the squirrelly guy had placed a new and improved Mick in the mayor's office.

He looked around the dreary acres. Trees were just skeletal remains. Only the tall evergreens stood like sentrys guarding the property.

Everything's dead now, Sara. Getting pretty chilly these days. All the leaves have dropped. And you know, you left me with the damn garden to clean up. Simon has depleted the freezer of every cake and pie. He blamed the cold for the tears forcing their way to the surface and the chilly air for the ache in his chest.

The flowers on Ada's grave were yellow and brittle and Dagger shook the thought that had always been in the back of his mind...that Sara was lying dead somewhere, her body as dried out as the flowers.

Einstein misses you. We miss you. Things just aren't the same. Can't find one damn file. He pressed his fingers to his eyes, the pain of loss almost unbearable. There were days he had to fight the anger, anger at her for not communicating, not easing his mind by at least letting him know she was alive. Anger for her leaving his life just as mysteriously as she had entered it.

He drew his legs up to his chest and pressed his forehead to his knees. The cold wind bit against the back of his neck and he pulled the blanket tighter.

Dammit, Sara. He blinked wearily, peeking over his knees at the creek below. Maybe it was the rush of water over the rocks or the wind rippling through the naked branches. But he could swear he heard a voice in his head. And this time it said:

I need some time.

END

NOW IN PAPERBACK

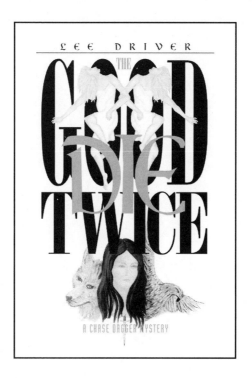

The Good Die Twice
The 1st Chase Dagger Mystery
ISBN 0-9666021-5-3
$6.50

A man receives a phone call from his wife.
Only one problem: She's been dead for five years.

About the Authur

Lee Driver is the pseudonym for mystery author Sandra Tooley. A former casino dealer, Sandy has also worked as a technical writer and a seminar coordinator. She has written numerous short stories, in addition to her Sam Casey series. *Full Moon-Bloody Moon* is the second in her Chase Dagger series. The short story prequel by the same name was published in Rosewort, an on-line, Internet horror magazine. A native of the Chicago suburbs, the author is a member of Mystery Writers of America, Sisters in Crime, and the National Museum of the American Indian. When not writing or traveling, the author can be found on the golf course.

The author can be reached at:

www.sdtooley.com
ChasenHts@aol.com